# BY JASON PARENT

The creature sailed into the trees before them. Abigail and KY veered left and ran even harder. Those awful things, those monstrosities, scurried like rodents across their path. KY booted one, and it sailed like a soccer ball into a far-off goal. Abigail sidestepped one, then another, wondering how long she could keep it up.

KY seemed to be running with a purpose beyond the obvious life-or-death stakes. He ran toward something. What did he see? What lay ahead?

A light glinted over his shoulder and was gone. Abigail wondered if she had imagined it, but it returned, again and again, each time KY's shoulder dropped.

*Is that a cabin?* The light was rectangular. It was ethereal, a fragile portal offering hope and safety shrouded by dying leaves and scraggly branches. She saw no yard between her and it—just death and worms.

Still, Abigail strained to reach it. What other hope of escape did she have? Her legs wobbled beneath her, a dull ache running through every inch of them. She had pushed them far beyond their limits, and yet, she asked more of them.

They had no more to give. Less than a hundred yards from the cabin, her legs failed her. She fell. Her hands and face slid along wet earth.

*I'm sorry, Karl. I should have been kinder.* One of those slug monsters landed on her back, tearing and gnashing.

White-hot pain seared through her muscle. The thing had latched onto her back like a wet suction cup against a glass surface. She felt something tugging at her arm and tried to pull away, but KY latched on, too. He helped her to her feet. His sheer will was enough to force her forward.

*Karl, you stupid fool. You ignorant, fat, heroic, mindless savior.* She could have kissed him then, if she hadn't been screaming.

Copyright ©2018 by Jason Parent
ISBN 978-1-63789-715-7
Macabre Ink is an imprint of Crossroad Press Publishing
All rights reserved. No part of this book may be used or reproduced in any manner
whatsoever without written permission except in the case of
brief quotations embodied in critical articles and reviews
For information address Crossroad Press at 141 Brayden Dr., Hertford, NC 27944
www.crossroadpress.com

Crossroad Press Trade Edition

# CHAPTER 1

He let out a breath. It rose like smoke from a burgeoning fire, obscuring his view through the scope for only a moment—an opportunity for escape that his target squandered.

*Aim. Breathe. Shoot.* The words were his mantra, spoken in the voice of the man he had once called "Father," though he had never earned the title. No, his father had left him half a lifetime ago.

His mark remained somewhere in the woods, toiling where his father's grim teachings haunted. Those teachings included how to use a Remington Model 798: how to clean it, how to carry it, and most of all, how to shoot it. With his father, missing had never been an option.

*Aim. Breathe. Shoot.* He would not miss.

The rifle's barrel rested along a waist-high boulder. Tyler crouched behind it, hidden in tall grass and the shade of suffering, brown-leafed hickory trees. Behind him, a large lake sat silent and still, black as death. Even the orange glow of the early morning sun shrank away from its glossy, opaque surface. Giant reeds jutted from its shallows, stabbing like spears at the sky.

In his youth, he had found the sweet-sappy smell of the trees inviting. The pines still stood tall, but those near the lake no longer thrived.

Wildlife usually set up base camps around the many watering holes of Kansas, but not this lake. The animals seemed to sense that its waters weren't for drinking. The lake was stagnant and putrid, a festering pit of water as black as oil and home only to snaking weeds and buzzing parasites. An almost toxic odor, like that of fish rotting under hot sun, rose from it, so pungent that the trees could not filter it. Instead, thirsty roots drank the poison greedily, and the water consumed them back, rotting them from the inside out like decaying teeth. Their leaves looked starved and shriveled, and their trunks were splitting and cracking, revealing sick and crumbling hearts.

Tyler peered through the scope. The rifle's cold metal shaft foretold the bullet's trajectory. He scanned the head of the trail. It opened like a river into a delta of dirt and grass.

He held his breath. The sound of bodies in motion— swishing through branches and bounding through brush— reached Tyler's ears. The sound grew louder.

Movement flashed across his peripheral vision. Tyler would not break his position. *You take the shot you're given, not the one you think you can get.* Good ol' Dad had taught him that, too, before abandoning him to the whims of the world. He'd taught Tyler plenty else, like pain and punishment, hatred and fear. Yeah, good ol' Dad was a real ol' asshole.

But he was gone. So why was Tyler so afraid?

*Aim. Breathe. Shoot.* His father's voice, always cold, echoed through his head. He flexed a finger across the trigger. Glimpses of life, barely more than shadows, zigzagged in and out of his line of fire. A blurred mass of pale-brown fur, speckled white, hopped toward the trail, the tall grass a barricade that was soon to be breached.

The deer leapt into sight. Tyler hesitated for half a second, let out his breath, and took the shot. The bullet roared from its chamber, shattering the tranquility of the moment.

Screaming. Too much screaming. A creature writhed in agony. It was not the deer.

Horror set in. Tyler's lips quivered. His mouth hung open. He didn't believe—couldn't believe—what he'd done.

"Please," a young man cried. "Help... me."

The words slapped Tyler out of shock. He raced toward his victim, who lay near the mouth of the trail not more than twenty yards from Tyler's hiding spot. Blood trailed behind the young man, his momentum causing it to spatter wildly across the grass—more blood than Tyler had ever seen.

Tyler recognized the young man from school. He'd been a

senior when Tyler was a freshman. His name was Stevie, and he had to be about twenty years old. His hair was darkened by sweat and matted as if he'd been wearing a cap. His skin was a pale, ghastly white, and his eyes were glazing over. Tyler couldn't meet them.

From a hole in Stevie's jacket, white stuffing turned red as it absorbed his blood like a cotton ball in dye. It saturated quickly then hung like wet hair around the wound. Tyler had seen bullet holes before, and this one looked bad. It passed through the top of Stevie's chest, just under the shoulder. Tyler's knowledge of anatomy was questionable at best, but he guessed that he had missed all vital organs. Stevie might yet live, if only Tyler could find him help.

Except Stevie had other wounds. Grotesque mutilations marred his frame. Thick strips of flesh were separated from his limbs and back along with pieces of his clothing, baring his ligaments and bones. Compared to these wounds, the bullet hole was an afterthought.

"Oh God, please help me," Stevie begged. He reached toward Tyler. The young man's thumb and forefinger were missing, nothing left of them but dirt-encrusted stumps. His eyes rolled back then returned with renewed vigor. The boy wanted to live.

"We have to get out of here!" he shouted as he tried to stand, his mangled hand grasping for assistance.

Tyler wondered why Stevie didn't let go and die. Whatever horrors had been enacted on him, he wouldn't survive them. Maybe it was that attack itself—the unfairness, the brutality—that made him fight to live. Despair ate its way through Tyler's core like a grave worm. He couldn't help. Still, guilt urged him to try. It was partly his fault that Stevie was dying.

He held Stevie down. "We need to put pressure on that wound. You're losing too much blood."

Tyler pressed his palms over the entry wound, not knowing if he was helping or hurting. He cursed himself for not having a cell phone, never having needed to call anyone before. Stevie winced, his eyes rolling back again, eyelids fluttering. Blood ran through Tyler's fingers. He glanced around him as if emergency medical supplies might magically sprout from the earth. He found nothing to avail him. The situation was worsened by the fact that they were at least a mile into the park. The ranger station at the entrance was their nearest and best chance to find help.

Stevie was going to die. Tyler wondered if he should aid his passing. The thought sickened him. He had done enough already to speed along Stevie's death.

Tyler looked down at Stevie. The young man's eyes stared back at him. A moment of clarity shone through them.

"You don't understand," Stevie said between coughs. He pawed at Tyler's shirt, his fingers catching in a breast pocket and pulling him closer. Blood trickled from the corner of his mouth. He was trembling. The front of his pants dampened. "We have to run. We have to escape…"

The words trailed off as Stevie's eyelids began to close. Again, they shot open, Stevie fighting to remain conscious. His gaze darted about the treetops, looking past Tyler as if the person who'd shot him was of no concern.

Stevie's battle was nearly over, Tyler realized. His blood stained Tyler's hands and caked his jeans. Stevie had lost too much of it.

Then, with a scream, Stevie bolted upright as if possessed by a demonic spirit. He knocked Tyler aside, pushed himself to his feet, and ran. But he didn't get far. After only a few steps, he fell face-first into the dirt. He didn't get back up.

Crying, Tyler knew there was nothing left to do. Stevie wasn't moving, not even the slight rise and fall of a diaphragm. He was gone.

Tyler stumbled back to civilization, not remembering how he got there. At the park entrance, he found a family of four unloading camping supplies from their minivan, not noticing the bloodstained boy until he had gotten within shouting distance and one of the children screamed. Tyler asked the father if he could borrow his phone. The man leaned back into the van, keeping his distance, but he pulled a cellphone from his back pocket and tossed it to Tyler while the mother ushered their two children away.

Tyler dialed 9-1-1. A woman's voice, soft and soothing,

answered. She asked him to state the nature of his emergency.

"I just shot someone," was all Tyler could mutter. He was still sobbing when the police came and escorted him away.

# CHAPTER 2

*Six years.*

*Six fucking years. Gone, just like that.*

Tyler had called Wichita State Penitentiary home long enough to miss the outside but not long enough to forget it. Not that there was anything left out there for him.

He was leaving prison just as he had entered it: alone. His mother had been his only real connection in the eight years preceding his sentence. He had told his classmates his father had gone to Florida where he was making it rich, the reality being far less glorious. In fact, the truth was a bitter pill. His dad was gone. As Tyler grew a little older, he had come to prefer to leave it at that.

Time without his father had proven to be a better, safer scenario until he had found himself in prison. But Tyler could never really escape the man's influence. Sure, his father had taught Tyler how to hunt, camp, and fish. He'd even bought Tyler his first bicycle. When it was stolen from the local convenience store because Tyler forgot to chain it up, his father gave him his first whipping. They came more regularly after that. Sometimes, good ol' Dad removed his belt for other reasons.

Tyler had hated the man—still did. For all the times his father had beaten his mother, Tyler couldn't understand why she didn't hate him, too.

He loved his mother, but she was weak. She had always been a heavy drinker, but after Dad vanished, fish could have taken a lesson or two from her on how to guzzle down liquid. When her only child went to prison, she hit the bottle harder than a rock star. With Tyler no longer around to look after her—to carry her to bed when she did a face-plant on the kitchen floor, to hold her hair back when she vomited their spaghetti dinners, and to make sure she even ate at all or brushed her teeth or took a bath—she drank herself to death less than two years into Tyler's sentence. Her funeral earned him his only time out.

And now the powers that be told him it was time to go home. He was out on parole for "good behavior." What behavior was that—not causing a stink every time a fellow inmate brutalized him? *You're welcome, Kansas.*

And what home? As far as he knew, his mom's trailer had been repossessed. He didn't want to live there anyway, not with all the bad memories that crowded it. He'd never had any real friends, and the few delinquents who had passed through his life before the shooting—those who'd hung around Mom's trailer and taught him how to lie, cheat, and steal to survive— were long gone by sentencing.

He had nothing except the clothes the prison had provided him: an ugly plaid, button-down shirt two sizes too small, with his six-foot frame threatening to bust through the seams, and some black Levi's that hung off his hips. Tyler was glad he didn't have to wear his old clothes. He hoped they had been burned. Every time he thought of his old T-shirt and jeans, he could still see Stevie's blood on them. Sometimes, he still saw it on his hands.

Prison had hardened him physically, and his body was thin but toned, chiseled from a combination of boredom and necessity. He wondered if it had strengthened him inside. He had spent every day afraid, so much so that fear had become routine. Now, as he stood at the gate, waiting for the guards to buzz him through, Tyler was afraid to leave.

*You'll never amount to anything,* his father's voice chided in his mind. *You're nothing but a loser.* Another, softer voice chimed in, and Tyler knew it to be the voice of reason. *There's nothing out there for you.*

Except, perhaps, closure.

For six long years, Tyler had done whatever was necessary to survive, even while questioning whether he deserved to live. Six continuous years of absolute hell: ass-fucking, shank-making, grub-guarding, yard-beating, pillow-biting hell. Prison had not been easy for a fair, slender boy of sixteen, easy prey thrown into a den full of predators. Yeah, the things he had seen, the things he'd *done*, might have made him tougher. They'd definitely turned the chip on his shoulder into a whole bag of Doritos.

And as hard as his fellow inmates had been on him, Tyler's hours alone in prison had been even worse. His thoughts would always return to the act that had put him into the slammer. Six years of dwelling on that day had dug a hole inside him.

He was walking out of Wichita State a man, all grown up but empty inside. Broken.

Maybe he had always been like that. He'd been a screwed-up kid when he had pulled the trigger and shot the bullet that the law deemed responsible for ending Stevie Coogan's life. Before that, he'd tried every drug he could get his hands on, and he could steal a car before he could legally drive one. Before shooting Stevie, Tyler's blatant disregard for authority and civility had thrust him into his fair share of scuffles and more than a handful of run-ins with the law, but never anything serious, never anything that stuck.

Nothing like *murder*.

That was what the good Christian state of Kansas had called it. The case against Tyler had rested entirely upon the bullet. There was no question that Tyler had shot Stevie, but the cause of death had been about as certain as a weather forecast made by a groundhog. The prosecutor had submitted various medical reports to muddle the issue. So-called experts had claimed that the bullet wound was a contributing factor to Stevie's death or an intervening cause or some other horseshit.

As flimsy as the testimony had been, the physical evidence hadn't lied. The pictures of the corpse had shocked the court. Someone leaked them to the local news. Stevie looked as though he had been butchered alive. His bones had stayed intact, mostly, but lengths of flesh and fist-sized chunks of muscle had gone missing. No known animal could have caused that kind of mutilation, at least not anything indigenous to Kansas. With one dead and three missing, the whole damn county had wanted answers—or at least someone to blame.

Cherokee County had never found its answers. It had never found the three missing twenty-somethings, either. For weeks, search teams had scoured every inch of Galveston State Park, delving far to the east into the Ozark Plateau and the foothills, and west, well beyond the lake. They never found more than their own footprints.

But the county had found its scapegoat. By the time of Tyler's plea hearing, local news and upstart politicians had called for his head. The victim's family and those of the missing had led the crusade. They had needed a villain, a target for their hatred, sadness, and confusion. They needed to assign blame where there was none.

No one had believed Tyler's story—that he had been hunting deer when a blur, nothing more, passed in front of his gun just as he fired it. Tyler hadn't expected them to. The only one who could have spoken the truth lay in pieces upon a cold metal slab in the county morgue.

Foolishly, he had believed that the state's inability to prove he had caused Stevie's other wounds would absolve him. His lawyer, a public defender named John or James or Jason, had disagreed. Charged with first-degree murder, ignorant of the woeful failings of the American justice system and having less cash in his pocket than a tourist walking down the wrong street in Wichita after midnight, Tyler relied upon the advice provided him. He had pled "not guilty" and was thrown back in jail anyway.

Later, after Tyler had spent a month twiddling his thumbs in the county jail, his attorney paid him a visit. He convinced Tyler that pleading out to a charge of manslaughter was his best bet. As the public defender had explained, the state was anxious to hang someone for the crime and would leap at the chance to place even part of the blame on any poor victim who would volunteer. They were offering a plea: manslaughter, with three years recommended sentence—a deviation from the normal sentencing range based on Tyler's youth. He would spend the rest of his childhood, two and a half years tops, in a juvenile detention center, followed by a year of parole, with the possibility of time off for good behavior. The alternative was to be tried as an adult for murder and, if found guilty, sentenced to a life in prison. Even an involuntary manslaughter conviction could have netted him fifty-five months of prison time.

He entered his guilty plea to the crime of manslaughter, thinking his sentence would be exactly as his lawyer had promised. The judge accepted it.

But "recommended," Tyler learned, did not mean *guaranteed*. Contrary to popular belief, a judge could accept a plea but impose whatever sentence he or she chose, regardless of whatever promises the prosecution might have made, so long as the punishment suited the crime. Apparently, Judge Fucktard didn't feel the agreed sentence was punishment enough. No doubt pressured by outside forces, he altered Tyler's punishment to fit the sentencing guidelines for adults convicted of manslaughter: a minimum of eighty-seven months in Wichita State Penitentiary, an ungodly place where only the strong survived, with instructions to "take it or leave it." The latter meant he'd have to face the first-degree murder charge, which his lawyer told him he had no chance of beating. Tyler took the deal.

Stevie's family cried foul. So many of them were present at the sentencing that Tyler couldn't hear the judge over their outbursts. They threw insults his way, then objects. Some promised their own brand of justice.

One remained silent, a pretty girl in pigtails who was a few years younger than Tyler. She had sparkling blue eyes made ugly by a cold stare full of hate. On seeing the condemnation in those eyes, Tyler's façade of strength crumbled. He felt so guilty beneath the girl's stare, even though he knew Stevie would probably have died regardless of the bullet wound. *I didn't kill him*, he silently pleaded to that girl's blue eyes. He couldn't rationalize away his shame. He didn't even believe it hadn't been his fault.

The judge banged his gavel. Order did not return. As two pro-wrestler-sized court officers shuffled him from the courtroom, Tyler's eyes filled with tears. They fell not for his loss but for the loss he had caused the girl whose stare siphoned away the last remaining bits of his soul. He couldn't avert his eyes from her, and she wouldn't take hers off him.

Those mad blue orbs had followed him from the courtroom. They followed him still.

He felt the girl's stare as he stepped through the prison gate. He saw it every night in his dreams and hoped never to see it again in the flesh. That would be another nightmare in a life already plagued by them. Somehow, he had survived prison, a fact that amazed him but did not necessarily please him.

*Out of the frying pan.* Tyler still felt as though he needed to constantly look over his shoulder. He shrugged. *Now what?* Funny... he hadn't really considered what came next for him until that moment.

He thought of nothing beyond the lake.

He took in the fresh air but still smelled the air inside, his nostrils filling with musk. He looked to his right, then to his left. Empty cars lined the parking lot. The prison loomed behind him like a gothic castle, walling off those inside as if *they* were in need of safeguarding from the regular folk. Its gates beeped shut.

Tyler sighed. The $42.56 he had in his pocket from doing prison laundry would only get him a cab ride across town and a sandwich, if he was lucky. His past—everything he once had and everyone he once knew—was gone. Yet the memories he wished he could erase lingered.

A beat-up Chevy Malibu with no hubcaps pulled up while Tyler pondered his next move. An unintimidating man in his mid-fifties, wearing black slacks, a white button-down shirt, and a thin black tie that crumpled over a slight potbelly, stepped out of the car. An encyclopedia salesperson, if Tyler had to guess. Maybe he was there to stock the prison library.

Tyler started walking. Whoever the man was, he didn't concern him.

"Sorry I'm late," Encyclopedia Man said.

Tyler stopped and faced him.

"There's always a fire to put out back at the ranch." The man scrunched his forehead, adding wrinkles to the wrinkles. "You're Tyler, right?"

"Who wants to know?"

The man laughed. "You guys are all the same when you get out. I'm Charlie Jackson, your parole officer. Didn't they tell you I'd be picking you up today?"

"Must not have gotten the memo."

"Well, come on. Get in. Let's get you to your new home. It isn't much, but I'm sure it's a heck of a lot better than your last residence." He nodded toward the prison. "I'll explain everything on the way over."

As he patted Tyler on the shoulder, Tyler shied away from his touch. He couldn't recall a time when physical contact had been a positive thing.

"I don't have to go anywhere with you."

"No? You've got a better option? There are no halfway houses in our fine state, but lucky for you, I've got the closest thing to it. I own a few rental properties and have this unfortunate habit where I go out of my way for unfortunate souls looking to get back on their feet. And the best part for the both of us is we won't have to go over to Pittsburg for you to report in to your parole officer." Charlie sighed and gave him space. "You can relax," he said as if trying to pacify a toddler. "You're going to need friends out here now. As lame as it sounds, I want to be your friend."

"You some kind of queer?"

If Charlie was offended, he didn't show it. "Nope. Just someone who truly wants to help."

"Why would you want to help me?"

"Because I've been where you've been, stood where you're standing. If someone hadn't helped me, I would have ended up right back inside. It's hard walking the Lord's path, especially for someone who has fallen so far from it."

*Great, a Jesus freak.* Tyler slowly released his breath. *Freedom's starting with a bang.*

"You don't have to believe in Him," Charlie said as if sensing Tyler's cynicism. "And I can't speak for Him and claim that He believes in you. But I believe in you. If I could change, anyone can. Okay, enough self-esteem building for one day. Let's get you home."

He opened the car door for Tyler. Waving an arm, he ushered him in.

A faded yellow Geo Tracker burst to life at the end of a row. The car stuck out like a priest at a whorehouse, but Tyler only just then noticed its occupant. A woman sat behind the wheel. Her blonde hair was tied back into a ponytail. Dark sunglasses hid her eyes. She seemed to be staring at him and Charlie from behind those lenses, but he couldn't be sure.

*Probably the daughter of the next guy getting released today. At least he's got somebody who gives a damn.* Still, something about the woman made him look twice, though he couldn't put his finger on it. He shook it off and got into Charlie's car.

Before Charlie could take his seat, tires screeched against pavement. Tyler turned toward the sound just in time to see the Tracker speeding away. The driver rounded a corner and was gone.

"Kids," Charlie said, shaking his head as he plopped down behind the wheel. "Always rushing through life, never taking the time to appreciate the everyday miracles around them."

Tyler was only half listening. As Charlie pulled the car away from the concrete fortress, Tyler stared absentmindedly out the window. His thoughts, as always, drifted back to the day when he shot a young man then fast-forwarded to that hostile girl with a stare made of hellfire and vengeance. He had been condemned by the power behind those eyes, his damnation reflected in them. Even now, the image chilled his soul.

# CHAPTER 3

"You ready for round three?"

Hearing the playfulness in Sebastian's voice, Jeanette knew he was ready. And so was she.

She no longer cared that she was having an affair or that they were out in the middle of nowhere, sucking and fucking in the dirt like animals. The twinge of guilt she'd once felt when she thought of her husband, Todd, at home with their two children while she took a "girl's getaway" with her made-up friend and coworker, Sally, was a distant memory. Sebastian made her forget all of that. The sex was *that* good. No, it was fucking amazing. Sebastian turned sex into an art. He'd opened her up in ways she'd never imagined she could open.

*How many orgasms has he given me?* She'd lost count after a dozen, one flowing right into another, all control forfeited. She loved every goddamn minute of it. Todd didn't know a clitoris from a kneecap. He certainly didn't know how to please or tease one. *Slobbering idiot.*

Jeanette never had to fake it with Sebastian. She would leave it all for him—her home, her family—if only he'd ask.

Her entire body ached. Her legs trembled, and although the night air was cool, temperature had nothing to do with her shaking. A cramp twisted her stomach. She wondered how many times Sebastian had speared her. Yet she was still wet, always wet for him, always craving more. She felt like such a whore, and it excited her. She was ready for round three.

*Pace yourself, you slut*, she told herself. *You're not as young as you used to be.* But damn, she felt young, as though she was back in those five college years that she had spent on ecstasy and dick, popping pills and popping off orgasms as if that was what college was all about. Todd had no idea about any of that, either. *Useless boy. I never should have married him. If he didn't have money and that sweet ride...*

Feeling young again—that was what Jeanette liked best about her new boy toy. Sebastian seemed to crave her as much as she did him. The way his cock hardened at her touch told her that she was still beautiful, still desirable, and that was the sweetest fruit, her fall into Eden.

"Someone's waiting for you."

Jeanette turned to see his purple-headed warrior—and if ever there was a penis deserving of that term, it was Sebastian's—poking out through the tent zipper. She giggled and covered her mouth with her hand. Though nothing they had done, however wild, had made her blush, his silly joke did.

Her smile curled mischievously. *Already hard.* "I'll be right back. I just have to use the little girl's room."

"You can do it on me if you want."

"Gross! You're so dirty," she said, laughing. "You sure know how to get a girl back in the mood."

"Please hurry." Sebastian clicked on a light inside the tent. She could see his dark outline through the tent's thin red mesh. His hand was oscillating up and down just below his waist. "I'm not sure how long I can wait for you."

Jeanette rolled her eyes. Sebastian's T-shirt, as big as a nightgown on her frame, slid down one arm. A late-spring breeze blew across her naked shoulder, sending chills down her spine and cooling the sweat between her breasts. She crossed her arms and stiffened as she walked across the dew-covered clearing to where the vegetation thickened. The wet grass and soft earth caressed the spaces between her toes. The air smelled clean, a refreshing change from the exhaust fumes and sewer-pipe stink of the city.

Her nostrils flared as she drew the crisp air into her lungs. Pure oxygen—mostly. Something foul lingered, barely detectable. She sniffed her armpits, assuming the odor to be a byproduct of her sexual athletics.

*I can't go home stinking like this.* She frowned. She didn't want to go home at all.

She gazed up at the stars. They had already lost some of their twinkle. Just above the treetops to the east, the black of night faded to gray. Though she couldn't see it, she imagined it faded even more at the horizon. Purples and pinks would follow, then the oranges and reds of the sun's first rays. Had she really fucked the whole night through?

Her body would pay for it, but she'd worry about that later. Carefully, she stepped into the brush, mindful of twigs and thorns. Out of habit, despite the isolated location, Jeanette felt the need to hide herself while she urinated. She took a few steps into the darkness beneath the trees.

A bush shook a few feet in front of her. Jeanette yelped and rocked back on her heels. She froze and listened. Something dashed away, disturbing the undergrowth as it traveled. The racket suggested something larger than a squirrel—a fox or large rabbit, perhaps, or maybe even a coyote or small bear.

The mental image of claws and teeth brought with it a wave of anxiety. She'd read the signs on the way in that basically said, "Hey, stupid, don't feed the bears, or they might feed on you." And if a black bear cub was around, Mommy and Daddy bear could be close by, too.

Coyotes didn't sound much better. They might as well be wolves. Jeanette didn't know anything about the canines or if they even lived in the Ozarks. She had heard stories about coyotes stealing babies and eating them. Or were those dingoes? She wasn't sure. She wasn't even sure she knew what a dingo was, but she knew she didn't want one next to her in the middle of the woods while she tinkled around her ankles.

*If it's a bear, play dead. If it's a coyote… run like hell.*

Her eyes followed the sound, but she couldn't see its maker. Whatever it was had stopped moving no more than twenty yards off.

"I'm waiting," Sebastian called. "What's taking so long?"

"Shush!" Jeanette spat. Her heart was racing. For the first time in their three-day woodland weekend, she remembered why she hated the great outdoors. Camping was Sebastian's thing. Sebastian was hers. Had Galveston State Park not afforded such convenient seclusion, she wouldn't have gone out there unless she were bound, gagged, and dragged by her feet. She had already experienced two out of three of those things that evening. Her thoughts shifting, she began to relax.

Until the noisemaker moved again. This time, it came a foot or two closer.

"There's something out here." Jeanette spoke loudly, hoping to scare the animal away.

She could almost hear Sebastian sighing. "Babe, we're in the middle of the woods. There are a ton of things living out here. None of them will hurt you. It's probably just a rabbit. It's perfectly safe."

"Yeah, but it's still here. I think… I think it's watching me."

Jeanette couldn't explain it. A voice inside her told her that whatever it was, she should be afraid. It was watching her—watching and waiting. But for what? She tried to chalk it up to irrational fear, but synapses inside her brain flashed a repetitive warning. The hairs on her arms rose. She stood silent, listening for another sound, scanning the area for whatever forest creature was standing its ground nearby, and terrified by the thought of finding it.

But Jeanette couldn't see a damn thing except dirt and shrubs and trees. The moon lit up the clearing as if it were under a protective dome. The lush firs, tall as skyscrapers, shrouded the forest in impenetrable night where anything could hide.

"Now who's killing the mood?"

Jeanette glanced over her shoulder to see Sebastian's proper head poking out of the tent. His carefree eyes and perfect smile grounded her, gave her courage. She blushed, feeling silly. An animal had fled from her, likely more afraid of her than she had been of it. She was the foreign presence out there, interrupting the creature's nighttime frolics. Nothing was out there but a cute, furry animal that had probably dove back into its home to escape her.

Nothing was watching her. She shrugged and smiled then pulled up her shirt and squatted.

"Cool," Sebastian said.

Jeanette exaggerated a frown. She was doubtful he could see it or her activity, but in the dead quiet of that sliver of time between the nocturnal creatures tucking in for morning and the birds singing to greet it, he could probably hear the flow of her stream.

"Get back in there," she ordered, scolding him as if he were one of her children.

"Aw," he whined. "You never let me have any—"

His words were cut short. So was Sebastian. His head fell to the ground, bounced and rolled a few inches. Blood spurted from his severed neck. Something Jeanette couldn't make out moved over it, clogging the hole.

She gasped. Her bladder emptied.

She hadn't seen anything approach him. She hadn't even seen it chop her lover's head off. Before her were only shadows, swirling against a curtain of darkness.

Her survival instinct erupted, and she turned to run, stumbling in her haste. She fell onto the urine-wet earth. A sharp pain rang through her knee as it collided with a rock.

Noises came from both sides of her and behind her, swishing sounds like sidewinders skirting over sand. They grew louder, closer. Jeanette scrambled to her feet and sprinted into the woods.

Her panic caught up to her, and she screamed. Her mind struggled to process what her eyes had seen. One moment, Sebastian had been alive and well. The next, his head lay at his feet.

Bile rose in Jeanette's throat. She wished she could wipe the image from her memory, but her mind resisted, playing it back over and over again like a terrible song on repeat. She needed to focus. Something was out there. It had killed Sebastian. For all she knew, it wanted her dead, too. She ran harder.

Branches clawed at her skin. Thorns embedded themselves in her legs. Her thighs screamed. Pain shot through her soles with every rock and twig they landed on. It kept her alert and afraid. It kept her moving.

She listened for sounds of pursuit, but she could only hear the whine of her labored breaths and the snaps of branches beneath her feet. Still, Jeanette would not stop. She didn't know where she was heading, and it didn't matter so long as it was far away from that clearing.

She ran for what seemed like an eternity. Nearly blind, she managed to dodge the trees in her path, hurdle those that had fallen, and press forward unimpeded. For a moment, she again felt young, as if she'd returned to the athletic prowess of her high school days, but the illusion crashed into the loss of Sebastian. She might never feel young again.

The trees began to thin. Jeanette caught a glimpse of the horizon, its pink glow spreading like oil across water from the world's end. She prayed she was nearing a road, another campsite, anything resembling human occupation. The hope of salvation drove her forward. She barreled out into the moonlight.

Into the clearing.

*No.* She skidded to a halt. Had the darkness disoriented her so thoroughly that she had been running in circles? *There's no way.*

But the familiar red tent stood just where Sebastian had assembled it. The light inside it had been turned off. Sebastian's body was gone. Something else shifted in the tent. A wet sound, like a dog lapping water, came from inside. Jeanette found herself praying for coyotes. At least they were real, an enemy she could comprehend. Coyotes did not cleave heads from their rightful places.

The lapping stopped. The sound of fabric ripping followed. A shadow rose from the ground in front of the tent. A head, then shoulders, possibly human, emerged from an indeterminable base.

Jeanette back-pedaled as silently as she could. Her legs were trembling, but this time, neither the cold nor sex was responsible. As she crept backward, she threw her arms out to her sides for balance. The back of her right hand collided with a tree. Her fingers fumbled along the grooves in its trunk. She edged closer and spun against it, keeping the tree between her and the tent. She slid down the bark, scratching her back against it as she crumbled into a fetal position. She clasped her hands over her mouth to quiet her heavy breathing. Her teeth bit down into the soft flesh between her thumb and forefinger. Sweat and tears rolled down her cheeks.

Jeanette heard the metal teeth of the tent's zipper separating. Her lover's murderer stepped out. She dared not turn and look, for fear of revealing her position.

A low, guttural growl emanated from the direction of the tent. It broke in places, rhythmic but unsteady like the purr of an old lawn mower. A series of dull thuds, like rocks falling to the earth, bowled toward her, ever closer. Surely, he—*it*, whatever it was—had spotted Jeanette and was coming to kill her. She closed her eyes and clenched her jaw, burying her teeth deeper into her hand. She could not steel herself for what she knew would come, nor could she run. Her survival instinct had abandoned her. Only terror remained.

Quick movements rustled through shrubs and plants. Sebastian's killer had left the clearing. It was close now.

Jeanette waited, her eyes closed tightly. Silence. After a moment, she opened her eyes. She saw nothing but the forest. Her arms huddled close to her sides. She planted her palms into the grass-covered ground, ready to make a stand if need be.

But when an object slid over her right hand—something slimy and loathsome—her bout of strength proved fleeting. The contents of her stomach rose to her throat. Slowly, Jeanette willed her head to turn. Her eyes met Sebastian's, his stare empty and lifeless, his severed head carried along the ground by some unseen scourge.

A gurgling sound, like that sucker thing her dentist put in her mouth to drain saliva, came from the clearing, then from the brush at her sides. It was everywhere around her, even resonating from underneath Sebastian's head as it moved past her. When the sound came from a small mound in front of her, her mind screamed at her to stand and run, but her legs gave up.

The mound had appeared out of nowhere. Jeanette hadn't noticed it before she'd closed her eyes. When Sebastian's head propelled toward it, seemingly of its own accord, she saw that the mound was alive and moving. Black, shapeless masses, vibrating with energy, revolved around a growing heap. The last of her lover disappeared inside it.

More of the black creatures slinked across the undergrowth.

Others fell from the trees. They were thick, gelatinous globs resembling human livers, if human livers could extract themselves from their host bodies and exist and move as autonomous entities. Some were bigger. The creature that had crossed Jeanette's hand had left behind a sticky residue, congealed like the adhesive gunk that stuck new credit cards to paper. It reminded her of hot cum left in a shower drain.

They came from all directions. There must have been a hundred of them. Jeanette was surrounded. When another brushed against her foot, she tucked her body into a ball and prayed they'd go away. For the moment, they showed no interest in her but continued steadily moving toward the mound, amassing into a single being. Their bodies emitted a low hum as they vibrated.

The liver-blobs piled atop one another, and the mound grew quickly. It towered over her.

On hands and knees, Jeanette crawled away. She had barely reached the tree that had hidden her when her progress was halted. Something had her leg.

She looked back to see a black circle pulsating around her ankle. She cried out in pain as her captor constricted like a boa. Beneath the creature, her foot twisted at an unnatural angle. She screamed louder as her bone snapped.

The black blob stretched flat, one end reaching for the ground, the other ever tightening around Jeanette's ankle. She wrapped her hands around it, trying to wring it like a wet towel and pull it free. As her grip tightened, it secreted a mucus-like substance and slipped through her hands. She kept at it, but every time she managed to get a firm grasp, her tugging only strengthened its hold on her ankle. Like an elastic band pulled tight and twisted, it sank into her skin.

Before long, the creature was tearing at her ankle, either gnashing through it with teeth or claws she could not see or breaking through by virtue of its never-ending constriction. The pain was unbearable, like thousands of tiny razor blades shaving off layer after layer of tissue until they reached bone. It clouded her mind. She rolled onto her back, howling in her torment.

The other end of the blob arched and straightened like an inchworm along the forest floor. As it did, it dragged Jeanette in tow.

She struggled against the creature's will, knowing her life depended upon it. She turned onto her stomach, grasping at stems and clawing at the dirt, searching for a hold. Her left hand found a patch of grass, and she held on fiercely, but the grass uprooted. She threw it aside and dug her nails deep into the mud. Ten trenches marked her efforts, and they were growing longer.

At last, they stopped.

Jeanette flipped onto her bottom. Her mouth dropped open, and her chin quivered. She tried to scream, but her voice had abandoned her. The dark figure of a man, large and foreboding, his features hidden in shadow yet somehow familiar, stood over her. It looked like Sebastian, but it was not Sebastian.

*You ready for round three?* Sebastian's voice ran through her brain. At least, it sounded like her lover, but any playfulness that had been in Sebastian's voice when he had asked her that question earlier was lost in translation. Was the Sebastian thing speaking to her? Had this sinister doppelgänger stolen her lover's voice? Surely it wasn't Sebastian. It couldn't be.

"Sebastian?"

*What's the matter, babe? Am I killing the mood?*

The Sebastian thing began to shake then fell apart. The many black masses that had formed it fell upon Jeanette, engulfing her body as if submerging her in quicksand. She gasped for breath as they wormed their way over her.

When they began to feed, Jeanette found her lungs again. The last remnants of night filled with her screams.

# CHAPTER 4

Abigail stank like smoked ham gone bad. Sweat ran down her spine and pooled in her ass crack, darkening her gray sweat pants in the shape of a thong. She pulled up the bottom of her T-shirt and used it to wipe the sweat from her face. Raising her arm let loose a fiercer stench. She scrunched her nose, repulsed.

She had barely pulled the shirt away before salt was burning her eyes again. All she tasted was salt. She could have sworn she was sweating out a new ocean. Why were her lips so dry when everything else was so wet? Wet and sticky, a combination she despised.

An upside-down thong formed beneath her breasts and up through her cleavage. The blue vest that hung loosely from her shoulders, unzipped, had nearly been discarded along the trail more times than Abigail cared to count.

But that would be admitting her discomfort, revealing weakness. Her stubborn pride would not allow it.

*I fucking hate hiking.*

Her husband wasn't faring much better. She could see him struggling, though just like her, he wasn't going to admit it. The same sweaty thong formed on his ass, only his was much bigger. *Fucking fat ass.*

And what made everything infinitely worse was that the whole damn getaway had been his dumbass idea. "Let's hike the trails at Galveston," he'd said. "It'll be fun."

*Yeah, about as fun as using a pinecone for a tampon.*

KY—Karl Young—looked down at her from a few feet higher up the trail. His big brown eyes looked as dim as always. He flashed her a smile as phony as their marriage. She glared back at him. It had been a long time since she had stopped hiding her contempt.

*Fuck you, KY.*

For all the time she'd known him—from their days of fooling around in back seats and childhood bedrooms, back when his titties were still smaller than hers, to the rocky shoals of their present-day wedded bliss—Karl had always been called by the nickname. His dumbass friends were bad enough, but even his inbred, redneck family called him "KY." Never mind that "Karl" actually took less time to say. Not a day passed without Abigail wondering what had ever possessed her to marry him.

Wispy strands of brown hair colored red flittered in a welcome breeze where they weren't tied back into her ponytail or matted to her forehead. The morning was cool. The sun was just beginning to rise. Yet too many clothes and too many burdens, not only the material kind that fit in their overstuffed backpacks, made their climb difficult.

"You coming?" KY taunted. His smirk flattened, with lips pressed thin, his humor no doubt dampened by Abigail's lack of amusement. Their little excursion was meant to bring them closer, to rekindle what they once had, far away from the distractions—and the conveniences—of ordinary life.

At least that was what Dr. Richardson had intended. The reality was far different.

Up until then, Abigail had kept her mouth shut. Every near slip, every quip from KY, and every mosquito bite added to her frustration. She was a time bomb ticking ever closer to explosion.

It had started early. She had remained silent as KY had awakened her before any sound-minded person would start the day and drove them out to Galveston State Park.

*Tick...*

She uttered no protests as her beloved husband picked the hardest hiking trail to climb. It didn't seem to matter to him that neither of them knew a damn thing about hiking and had spent most of their weekends eating pizza in front of the boob tube.

*Tock...*

She stifled her criticism and locked away her voice as KY

wheezed and lugged his gelatinous ass up a path filled with steep inclines and loose rocks, his wife like a loyal dog at his heels.

*Tick...*

A gymnast in her youth, Abigail had been tone and limber, but her athleticism had since given way to the wear and tear of aging. On the brink of her thirtieth year, her legs had softened a bit as she spent her days in a cubicle, seated behind a computer, but they were still strong, and her will was stronger—stronger than that tub of KY, anyway. She let him lead, watching and waiting patiently as he acted out some macho fantasy, pushing himself to exhaustion.

Waiting for his inevitable failure grew tiresome. KY turned around, offering her that stupid, smug grin plastered over his stupid, fat face, and Abigail had to summon her restraint. She kept her cool, smiled a smug grin of her own, and nodded, all the while picturing herself hoisting one of those loose rocks high and smashing it into her husband's enormous melon head.

*Tock...*

"Right behind you." Although the words were hard to form, she said them convincingly, pretending to be a lot less tired than she actually was.

The bomb within her ticked on. Still, she did not blow.

An earsplitting shriek blasted through the trees, shocking Abigail out of her marital anxieties. The sound filled her with fear. She hadn't heard a human make such a sound since her days as a waitress when a coworker had dumped a gallon of deep-fryer oil on himself while cleaning the machine. It was the sound of intolerable agony, pure and simple. And it terrified her.

The hair on her neck stood on end. She chewed her nails. The sound seemed to pass straight through her, rattling her bones.

The scream stopped abruptly, as if a hand had been cupped over its maker's mouth. Or maybe it stopped because the screamer was—

*No.* Abigail didn't want to think it. Her mind searched for rational explanations.

"What the hell was that?" The concern on KY's face heightened her own. With a simple question, he had killed rational thought.

*How the fuck should I know?* Abigail took deep breaths and reined in her hostility.

"It sounded like a woman's scream," she said shakily, hoping KY would offer another, equally plausible explanation. Even as the words passed her lips, Abigail hated the sound of them. She knew, without a doubt, that what they'd heard was a woman in anguish. Her mind reached for causes. Things lived in the woods. Things with sharp teeth. She wanted no part of them.

She turned around. Circumstances had changed. Abigail had no more time for foolish pride. Sanity demanded she return home.

"It came from that direction." With one seemingly innocuous sentence, KY exposed her cowardice.

She stopped, but she could not yet turn and face him. Her shame was too great. When it passed, Abigail turned and saw KY pointing into the trees. The trail they stood on was hardly easy hiking, but where KY pointed, she saw nothing but thick forest, darker and denser the farther in she peered.

"Somebody might need our help."

Though she wanted to, Abigail couldn't argue with that. Her mind searched for a counter but came up with nothing.

KY raised his knee and placed one tannish-orange hiking boot, freshly purchased for their hike, off the man-made path and onto a bed of nature in all its wildness. Dying grass curved beneath his foot.

"Wait." Abigail yanked her husband back onto the trail by the strap of his green backpack. Her argument had formed.

"Slow down there, cowboy. You're always so bullheaded. Think it through. The park ranger told us not to leave the trail, not for any reason. People get lost in these woods all the time. Some of them never come out. You know that. If we go out there, whoever that was will not be the only person in need of help."

KY dropped his chin. He stared down the bridge of his nose at Abigail. "So we're supposed to just leave her? That's pretty heartless, Abby, but not all that surprising coming from—"

"Do you even know what direction that is, you stupid, stupid twat?" Abigail blurted out the question as fast as she could, not wanting KY to finish his remark. As mad as she was, she would have taken it to a new level had he gotten to the end of that sentence. The time bomb had ticked down to its final seconds. She already wanted to strangle him and might have tried if she thought she could get her hands around his double chin. Yes, she was afraid, and that was definitely *part* of the reason she didn't want to leave the hiking trail. The heroic thing to do was not the right thing to do, or at least not the smart thing to do.

KY stared at the sky. Abigail shook her head. She knew he was looking for the sun. The tall oaks and flowering dogwoods to the east and the hills beyond hid all but a pinkish glow.

"North?" His lack of confidence gave him away, even if he had guessed right. He shrugged. "Well, I don't feel right doing nothing."

"It's probably just some teenagers screwing," she said, though she didn't really believe that.

"That didn't sound like—"

"It doesn't matter. I'll just call the ranger station and... damn!" Abigail hit her cellphone against her leg. "No bars. That figures." She slid her phone into her pocket. "We can head back down and put an end to this awful idea of yours—"

"That's, like, an hour away. Help will never get here in time." He pouted. His voice went quiet. "You're giving up already?"

For a second, she almost pitied him. KY still loved her. She knew that. She just wasn't sure she loved him back. That twinge of pity compelled her to propose a second option, one she instantly regretted. "*Or,* we can keep going to higher ground. It looks like there's a place up ahead where we might have a better chance of getting a signal."

KY smiled, big and dopey. Abigail rolled her eyes.

"Fine," she said, huffing. "Let's keep moving, then."

# CHAPTER 5

Life outside prison was hardly a life at all. Charlie had set Tyler up with a room that was a half step up from his cell and made his mother's trailer look like the Ritz Carlton. The job at which Charlie had placed him, shoveling shit onto shingles at a greasy motel diner just outside Baxter Springs, was not worth the minimum wage he earned. Still, it was honest money, and he worked hard for it.

His twenty-third birthday was only two weeks away. Hard time had pulverized the boyish charm Tyler once possessed. Every now and then, his dusty hair, prominent chin, and bad-boy stare would still earn him a flirtatious glance from a waitress or customer, but more often, people seemed to back off from him as if he sent out a warning signal to leave him alone.

Though Tyler never truly understood why, Charlie had taken a shine to him. He expressed real interest in seeing Tyler "rehabilitated," whatever the hell that meant. Tyler viewed him as a sort of father figure, and why not? Charlie had shown more interest in him over the last two months than Tyler's parents ever had.

At first, Tyler wondered if Charlie might be into more than just his rehabilitation, but the guy never made a pass at him, nor did he ever have an unkind word. He was the first person in a long time to acknowledge Tyler's membership in that hopeless group known as the human race.

Charlie took it easy on him, turning a blind eye to his tardiness and cursing. He seemed to understand what ate away at Tyler, though Tyler never voiced it. When he just needed to talk to someone, Charlie listened. Tyler legally only had to report to him once a week, but soon, he began visiting him far more often than that.

Tyler more or less followed Charlie's rules, at least those that mattered. In living under Charlie's roof, he submitted himself to rules that were stricter than the conditions of his parole, particularly with respect to curfews. Of course, he didn't like them, but after six years of eating and showering on someone else's say-so, the rules were minor inconveniences. Tyler understood that they were designed to keep him on the straight and narrow. He kept to himself and ducked low enough for trouble to pass over whenever it came looking for him.

Tyler had heard most parolees talk about their parole officers with scorn and hatred. Most of the others in the house didn't appreciate Charlie's efforts on their behalf, as if the world owed them something after it had taken away their freedom as punishment for their crimes. Tyler didn't share their mind-set. The world owed him nothing. But what did he owe the world?

Sometimes, it felt as though he owed it everything.

It was Charlie who encouraged him to go back out there, to find closure. All those memories tormenting Tyler day in and day out were bad for his psyche. In six years, all he'd thought about was what had landed him prison. If his finger had been a nanosecond faster or slower on that trigger, Stevie would probably still be dead, but Tyler's bullet would not have been a "contributing factor." Why did Stevie have to be at Galveston State Park, running down that trail at that exact moment?

*Fate put us there.* Tyler never understood why he hadn't fought against fate. He needed to make sense of the event that defined him, and if he couldn't make sense of it, maybe he could at least move past it—if the world hadn't already moved past him.

God, he hated that fucking town. He hated that sheriff who called him a liar. He hated the park rangers who stood around, pretending nothing was wrong, doing nothing, letting him— just a boy with a rifle and no parental guidance—come and go as he pleased. He hated those fucking townsfolk who called for a lynching, damning him for the deaths of four people when he'd only shot one. And he hated the court for taking away six years of his life.

His hate left him bitter. Tyler wasn't worth shit. The people who'd called for his head, all self-righteous and God-fearing, weren't worth shit either. The difference between Tyler and them was that Tyler knew exactly how little he was worth.

The need to put the memories to rest nagged him to go back to Galveston State Park. Tyler's demons resided in that park. He had to face them, like it or not. He had to go back.

One Saturday afternoon in May, just after his breakfast shift ended, Tyler borrowed a vehicle from a stranger who didn't know he was borrowing it and made the forty-seven-mile trek to Galveston State Park. He'd taken cars before in his life but had never broken the conditions of his parole. As he drove the dusty, dead streets out of the city and picked up the interstate, open highway stretched before him through fields and prairies, lush meadows of Indian grass and big bluestem. Behind him, off in the distance, the Ozarks formed a bumpy skyline shrouded by clouds.

Out there, nature should have felt untainted, but a shadow of evil seemed to lurk everywhere, its presence strengthening the closer he got to the park. Tyler pulled into the parking lot in the midafternoon. Galveston State Park wasn't much to look at, not like it used to be when he was a boy. Cracks ran everywhere across the paved lot, weeds and roots sprouting from them. In the small picnic area just beyond the lot, the tables were in desperate need of repair, the wood splintering and covered in bird shit. To his right, at the end of the lot, the ranger station had withstood time's onslaught fairly well. Like a raised ranch, it sat on a partly aboveground foundation. A deck, smooth and worn, circled the square building, with stairs leading up to it on all four sides.

Beyond the picnic area and the ranger station, as far as the eye could see, was a dense forest of hickory and oak, an occasional dogwood disturbing the monotony. Here and there, the mouth of a trail broke the tree line. One trail led to the campground and the former game area beyond that. Others wound over hills and through valleys. Still others ventured into parts of the forest where few had ever been. And one trail led to the lake.

All of them guaranteed nature at its wildest.

From the entrance, it was a bit of a hike to the campgrounds down what had once been a drivable dirt path and was now overgrown and riddled with bumps and trenches. The treads of campers, trucks, and SUVs dug deep trenches along the sides of the path. The road humped, alive with brush, between the trenches. Tyler doubted the Honda Civic he had acquired for the trip would make it more than ten feet before it bottomed out.

The game range and the pond within it sat beyond the campgrounds. The range had been closed to hunting a few years prior to Tyler's incident, so he doubted anyone would be out that way. *Just as well.* He didn't want to be seen. He just wanted to be alone, forgotten.

He stepped out of the car, tossed the keys on the seat, and closed the door. He inhaled deeply, remembering the smells, sights, and sounds as he took in the scene. The parking lot was nearly empty. It was late May, and Tyler expected camping season to be in full tilt. He saw an Outback with an empty roof rack, a Wrangler with monster truck tires, a rust-covered pickup, and a black Elantra. Near the ranger station were two Jeep Cherokees with the words GALVESTON STATE PARK written across their doors. One was running.

Tyler's head turned at the sound of a screen door swinging open.

"If I'm not back before six," a wiry, thin man with an equally wiry beard said as he took the stairs of the porch two at a time, "go ahead and leave. Just leave the lights on so people know I'll be back."

The man hustled toward the idling Jeep. As he rounded the vehicle, his eyes met Tyler's and gave him the once-over. Tyler stared back and was wondering what he had done to arouse the man's suspicion when the concern faded from the park ranger's face. He tipped his small sombrero-like hat at Tyler, who nodded back. The ranger hopped into the Jeep and backed up in a hurry. He drove past Tyler and turned up the bumpy path toward the campgrounds.

*That's right, old man. Let me come and go as I please, just like your kind always did.*

Tyler started to follow when he noticed a yellow Geo Tracker parked at the other end of the lot. It hadn't been there a moment earlier. The driver stood on the far side of the car, leaning against it while smoking a cigarette. Tyler studied her back with the same scrutiny the ranger had applied to him, unsure why the vehicle or the girl gave him pause. He shook it off and headed toward the trail.

The entrance to the forest looked just as he remembered it though a little less colorful, less vibrant. The hinges on the open gate had rusted. The Smokey Bear trash can tops were sun-bleached and graffiti-riddled. Thickets with shark-fin thorns lined the roadside. The vibe wasn't welcoming. It felt more like, "Enter at Your Own Risk." A sign that said as much hung from the gate.

He headed through it. Dressed only in a T-shirt, blue jeans, and sneakers, and carrying nothing but his inner burdens, he began his long walk to the lake.

*Welcome home,* he heard his father's voice say.

As Tyler approached the campgrounds, he saw a large wooden sign standing guard at the entrance. *Good to see there's at least one thing different about this place.*

He walked up to the sign and ran his fingers along the etched wood as if reading braille. "The state of Kansas is NOT responsible for your safety," he read aloud, mimicking Judge Fucktard's voice and mannerisms. "Please exercise caution and camp responsibly. Dispose of cigarettes and trash in proper receptacles, and douse all campfires. Do NOT feed the wildlife. Violators will be prosecuted to the full extent of the law."

Tyler scoffed. *The state of Kansas has never given two shits about my safety.* He recalled all the times correctional officers weren't there when he needed them. And where the fuck was the good ol' state of Kansas when he shot a kid with a rifle he wasn't supposed to have in an area where he wasn't supposed to be shooting?

Oh, but the state was there after the fact. *Fuck Kansas.*

He dropped his head. Whether he'd deserved to be locked up or not, none of that mattered anymore. It was time to put an end to that part of his life. He wondered what might come after.

With his hands thrust into his pockets, Tyler plodded forward. Long, leafy branches shaded the path and kept him cool, the sun only peeking through here and there like beams from giant spotlights. He passed a few camping areas. They were as quiet as a cold night and looked unoccupied.

Music blasted up ahead. The song had something to do with pimping hos and keeping bitches in line. Tyler suspected he'd find a bunch of privileged white boys getting drunk and thinking themselves street thugs. When he came up to the site, his suspicions were confirmed. They were frat boys, Alpha Omega motherfuckers, the kind who thought all of life was a party. Someday, they would learn how wrong they were.

He tried to sneak by the college kids unnoticed. He'd made it halfway across the break in the trees that gave access to the clearing when he heard a voice. "Hey, man. We got beers. You want one?"

Tyler sighed. *Great. They want to be my friends. Like that'll end well.*

With a clear view of the camping area, Tyler saw one of those motor homes that were similar in size and shape to a short bus, the kind with a sleeping area that overhung the cab. A banner with three symbols that might as well have been written by aliens hung from its side.

A young man stood several feet away from him. He seemed to be about Tyler's age, but he was tall as a power forward and thick as an offensive lineman. His shirt clung tight around a barrel of a chest. Yellow-brown stains ran down the front of it, but he didn't seem to mind. Beneath those stains, Tyler made out an arrow pointing to the man's right and the words "I'm with Stupid" beneath it.

Each of his meaty fists surrounded a can of beer that looked as small in his grip as a roll of quarters would look in any normal-sized hand. Empties lay at his feet and littered the clearing, marking his territory. The boy belonged in a zoo, scratching his hairy ass and going apeshit for bananas.

A heavy weight smothered Tyler's shoulder. Fingers curled around his collarbone. Startled, he spun away, throwing up his hands in defense.

A cold, dripping aluminum can was shoved into one of them. "Here you go." A boy with small, beady eyes and a big, goofy smile marred with crooked teeth thrust a beer into Tyler's hands. He cupped his hands around Tyler's. The smell of an opened keg permeated from the boy's massive frame, an aura so thick it could cause secondary drunkenness.

He was the same boy as the one in the clearing. Tyler couldn't wrap his head around it. No one could move that fast and be in two places at once, unless he was not one but two people.

Tyler looked back at the clearing. There, one of two identical twins stood, belching as he finished the beer in his right hand. He wiped his mouth and laughed. "That trick gets them every time." The twin was wearing the same shirt as his brother, stained with the same mystery streaks, except his "I'm with Stupid" arrow pointed left. "Too bad we can only do it once to strangers."

"You should have seen his face," his brother said, laughing. He put his arm around Tyler. "Come on, man. It's all in good fun. Have a drink with us?"

Tyler immediately disliked the twins. They reminded him of those evil little bastards from a Dr. Seuss book his mom used to read to him—Thing One and Thing Two. Except they were all grown up—not any more mature, but a whole lot bigger.

Thing One, the twin who was chugging beer faster than a Hummer guzzled gasoline, downed his second can. "Frosh!" he yelled. "Get out here. We have a guest, and we need more beer."

"Yes, sir." A small boy with curly black hair and a baby face nearly tripped in his hurry to exit the camper. He carried a six-pack in each hand. When another frat boy who followed him out pushed him, the boy fell and skidded across the grass. The beer cans clanged against each other as they hit the ground.

A sinister smile ran across the second boy's face. He seemed older than the others, older than Tyler even, and he was undoubtedly the group's ringleader. His deep brown eyes smiled, too, failing to conceal a dangerous mind. He crouched near Frosh. "What do you say?"

"Sorry, master. I didn't mean to get in your way, sir." Frosh stood and ran over to Thing One. He pulled a beer from the six-pack and opened it for him.

"Well, I'll be leaving now." Tyler raised the beer, popped it open, and took a swig. It tasted like warm piss, but he swilled it anyway, not realizing until then how thirsty he had become. He walked over to the trash barrel and threw away the empty can. Forcing a smile, he turned to the frat boys and waved. "Thanks for the beer."

As Tyler left, Thing One and Thing Two giggled like a pair of preteen girls at a slumber party, but it was the other one, the one who had pushed the youngest and weakest of their lot into the dirt, who concerned Tyler. He swore he could feel the boy's eyes on him as he walked away.

But walk away he did. The inane hazing rituals of a college fraternity were not his problem. He passed a few more tents and another motor home before the trees began to huddle closer. The sparse rays of light that broke through them formed a haze that was almost tangible, like a dust cloud sprouting from an old cushion that was suddenly slapped. The road faded into a few lines of matted grass.

A rope barred his path. From it hung another, simpler sign: "No hunting," and below that, "No trespassing."

*Well, this is it.* He let out a deep breath but hesitated before taking another step. *What am I doing? There's nothing good here for me.* He looked back. A long way off, the sun illuminated the path like the light at the end of a tunnel. It looked peaceful—another mirage.

*There's nothing good for me out there, either.*

He pulled his watch—a scratched mess with a broken strap that a customer had left at the restaurant—from his pocket. It was just after four in the afternoon. It would be dark in a couple of hours. Light or dark, it didn't make much difference. He had nowhere else he needed to be. Charlie would feel differently, he knew, but Charlie was a long way off.

Tyler caught his reflection in the glass of the watch face. Dark stubble lined his jaw like a thin layer of moss. His eyes had deep shadows beneath them and had almost lost their blue completely. They were dead gray husks around pupils as black as pitch. Gazing into them was like staring down two loaded barrels. He blinked, and the illusion dissipated.

Tyler shoved his watch back into his pocket and pressed forward.

*It's not far from here.* He peered down the trail into darkness. He knew the woods would open up again about a quarter mile up if he veered left. A trail would spit him out at the lake, into the light of day.

*I should easily be able to make it back before sunset, if… if I puss out.* Tyler shivered. The thought of stumbling through the darkness to find his way back caused him more unease than facing his past.

He stepped over the rope and headed down the path. There, the grass and weeds were as high as his knees, a home for crickets and ticks and all sorts of skittering creatures he'd rather not think about. After ten minutes of cautious slogging, Tyler headed left. He might as well have left the trail entirely. The remnants of the path were all but gone.

*The lake's just ahead—where they say I killed Stevie Coogan.* He spat, feeling the old wound festering. His guilt was piled high like a cartoon sandwich, all starting that day, or maybe culminating that day. Combined with his anger, it drove him onward.

After another fifteen-minute hike, Tyler felt the ground beneath his feet softening. He saw an opening up ahead. The grass gave way to mud. Tall reeds swayed in a cool breeze that carried a rank, rotten odor. The sun, lower in the sky, bathed everything in an orange glow.

Tyler couldn't see where the mud ended and the water began. The water was silent. He couldn't hear a single splash from a fish or turtle, not a croak from a toad or even an air bubble popping at the surface. A steady hum of insect wings— the shrill whine of swarms of mosquitos as thick as snow in a blizzard—was the only sound entering Tyler's ears.

The lake had always been still as glass, if his memory served, but it hadn't always been so stagnant and ugly. Only unpleasant things lived beneath its surface. Only unpleasant memories were born there.

*It's poison.* Even the deer he'd had in his sights six years earlier wouldn't drink from it. As a kid, Tyler and his dad had visited the lake with a cousin, now moved away and mostly forgotten, who jumped into the swamp end of it on a dare. Tyler remembered vividly his cousin's screams when he had emerged, leeches clinging to his appendages like tails pinned on a crazed, hee-hawing donkey. By the time they had burned the last one off, the boy was as white as chalk.

His cousin never returned to those woods. Tyler wished he'd been smart enough to do the same. But he had never been afraid of ugly things.

He looked for the rock where he had propped his father's rifle six years before. He wasn't supposed to have the gun, but his father apparently didn't need it where he'd gone, so Tyler had kept it hidden behind his dresser. His mother never found it. She would have had to get her drunk ass off the couch for that.

As much as he wished he could pin the blame on him, Tyler knew it wasn't his dad's fault that he had shot Stevie. It took him years to accept that it was his own fault. For a while, he had even tried to convince himself that Stevie shouldn't have been there, but that never worked.

Tyler clenched his fists. Stevie wasn't the only victim.

The stroll down memory lane wasn't helping any, and night was coming. Soon, it would be just him and the dark.

He approached the spot where Stevie had died, the opening of a trail that led to parts of the forest few humans had visited ever since the lake went bad. His mind showed him crushed grass and blood spilled and spreading, saturating the earth. A hand shot up from a young man who was dying, his eyes wide and blank, not looking at Tyler but through him.

Tyler closed his eyes and squatted near the spot. When he opened them, Stevie's ghost had vanished. The memory lingered. He could still smell the blast, see Stevie's terror, feel the blood on his hands.

What was it Stevie had said? Tyler delved deeper into the memory. It wasn't hard. The day couldn't be erased, not with alcohol or drugs and certainly not with any psychological mumbo jumbo.

Tyler repeated Stevie's dying words aloud. "We have to get

out of here. We have to run. We have to escape."

He shook his head. He knew they weren't just the words of a dying man, delirious with pain. Tyler stood and walked toward the lake.

Rapid footsteps sounded behind him. As he turned, he barely caught sight of an object as it collided with his forehead. Blinding pain shot through his skull, ringing it like a tuning fork.

He fell onto his back. A shadow moved over him. He struggled to clear his vision, but the black stars floating before his eyes blended into darkness as consciousness left him.

Sleep came, and with it, the night.

# CHAPTER 6

"We're lost, aren't we?"

Abigail was fed up. She was tired and miserable. Her thighs burned. Her calves ached. Sweat and bugs and all the ungodliness of nature infested her beneath her soiled clothes. And it was all *his* fault.

She leaned against a felled oak to catch her breath, her hand planted on the bark. Something bit her, and she pulled her hand away, screeching. Four fire ants held on fast as she shook her arm violently. One by one, she flicked them off, wishing eternal damnation on each pest. She looked at the tree where hundreds of the ants scurried about. How had she not seen them?

*I'm in hell.* She wondered when, and why, everything had gone so wrong.

"You okay?"

Abigail let out a breath and turned to her husband. She no longer cared who won their silent competition. Did that mean she had lost? KY looked ready to collapse, as exhausted as she was. In his sad eyes, she saw that there were no winners in their battle.

"Well? Are we?" she asked.

"How can we be lost? We're still following the trail."

"Yeah, but *which* trail? This trail has more splits than a fucking bowling alley."

"Good one," KY said, his dopey smile returning for the first time in hours. "I got one: more splits than a gymnastics competition."

Abigail rolled her eyes. Sometimes, KY could be so utterly useless. He had led them into this mess, and like all his messes, it was hers to clean up.

"I knew we should have gone left at that last fork."

KY shrugged. "Do you want to go back? The last sign said the campgrounds were this way. Someone there should be able to direct us out."

"Aren't men supposed to have some internal compass or something?"

KY was smart enough not to respond.

*First smart thing he's done all damn day.* Abigail dug through the front pocket of her backpack. It felt heavenly just to get it off her shoulders for a minute. The knots of twisted muscle would need strong hands to loosen them. She let her mind drift back to her honeymoon, when a hot Spaniard had rubbed oil on her back inside a Barcelona beach cabana. The daydream faded, the pain came back, and she groaned.

After a moment, she found her cellphone. "No bars. Fucking reception sucks balls out here."

"What did you expect? We're miles away from the nearest tower. Hell, we're miles away from the nearest town. Ain't nothing but grass and woods and mountains out here. Well, technically, they're hills."

Abigail slapped her forearm. "And mosquitos."

"And limestone." KY's face brightened. "This whole area is rich in—"

Abigail flashed her husband one of her patented shut-the-fuck-up stares. "You. Are. Not. Helping," she said quietly, keeping her glare icy despite the fire burning behind it. "We should've just gone to Mushroom Rock. Less hills, less trees and less bugs, I'm guessing. And we wouldn't be fucking lost!"

"Relax. We're not lost. And besides, I got through to the park ranger earlier. He knows we're out here. When he doesn't see us moseying down the trail, I'm sure he'll come looking for us. And if we keep to the trail, we're bound to run into somebody."

"Really? Is that your theory, genius? And who the fuck says 'mosey'?" Abigail pressed her fists against her hips. "We have been hiking for nearly twelve hours, and we haven't seen one person."

"Well, we heard one." KY laughed uneasily.

*Yes, we did.* She studied her husband. Her fingernails dug

into her palms. *He didn't take us off the main trail on purpose, did he?* She fumed. The possibility was not only likely but certain. *That fat bastard! I bet he's still trying to play the hero. The fathead led us this way on purpose!*

After several deep breaths, she relaxed her hands. *No, even he couldn't be that stupid.*

"That was shortly after we got here, when it was still dark out," she said just to be sure. "It's already getting dark again, a whole day gone. Anybody who needed help out here has either already received it or isn't ever going to get it. Got it?" She zipped up her backpack, slung it over her shoulder, and started down the trail, but she turned before taking her second step. "And that includes us!" She punched KY in the arm.

He looked hurt but not from pain. He rubbed his arm and sulked. "What do you want me to do, Abby? What do you want me to say? That I'm sorry? I *am* sorry. I'm sorry for a lot of things."

*Oh my God.* Abigail could see defeat written all over KY, from his sagging shoulders and downcast eyes to his fidgeting hands and shuffling feet. He looked like a caged gorilla, huddled over himself. He wasn't exaggerating his hurt.

He was trying. That was worth something. She toned down her bitchiness. "I'm… sorry." KY raised his chin a little. "Bug spray?" she asked, again sliding the backpack from her shoulders. She took out the canister and handed it to him.

"Don't mind if I do."

*And the dopey grin returns.* With it, Abigail's discontent returned. She kept it at bay as well as she could by controlling her breathing.

"So what's the plan, Stan?" she asked, trying to make light of their dismal situation. She knew of only one reasonable course of action, but she would let KY continue his charade of leadership. Though she'd been unable to stomach him for longer than she cared to admit, Abigail would rather have been trapped in those woods at night with KY than with no one at all.

"We push on." KY's smile had faded. He appeared calm, but she knew he was trying hard to mask his worry. His anxiety leaked through every time he ground his teeth or started to hum.

Abigail readied herself for a long night. When KY had finished, she doused herself with bug spray until the canister rattled. She straightened her back and stretched her arms to the sky. Then she slapped her thighs and rubbed the muscles. "We ready?"

KY nodded. "Ready."

He took the lead. They continued down the trail, a gradual decline, until the last light of the sun vanished from the sky.

# CHAPTER 7

When Tyler woke, his head was still ringing. Sticks and leaves clung to his shirt. Mud streaked his skin and soaked through his clothes. Every part of him itched, but for some reason, he couldn't scratch himself.

The dull tones inside his skull began to fade, replaced by the chirps of crickets and the incessant droning of cicadas. Then came the croak of a bullfrog, followed by the clang of metal against metal: a blade being sharpened.

The smell bombarded him next—a rank, musty odor, thick with mold, like rotted wood. As his eyes began to focus, he saw that his other senses had not betrayed him. He found himself in some sort of cabin or shack with walls, roof, and floor all made of decaying plywood, the boards nailed together without craft and rusted nail heads jutting from every surface. It was a tetanus infection waiting to happen.

To his right, he saw nothing except a wall. To his left, a table stood against the wall, a solitary chair resting beneath it. Dust and cobwebs covered both, except for a small circle on the table where the room's sole light source—a battery-powered camping lantern, modern and out of place—shined away the dark.

Brown stains blotted the floor. They looked as if they had been there as long as the shack had. In a corner, hidden by shadow, a field mouse squeaked.

As his mind began to focus, Tyler evaluated his circumstances. He was standing, sort of. His toes scraped along the floor, drawing circles in the grime. His arms had been hoisted above him, suspended at the wrists by inflexible, cutting metal. He couldn't see behind him, where the clanging originated. A need to see its source, to see what sort of person had abducted him, made him swivel clockwise.

Twisting only caused his wrists to flare with pain. He winced and glanced up. Blood trickled down the length of his left arm to the elbow. His right wasn't much cleaner. Handcuffs bound his wrists. A rope looped around the chain and ran over a crossbeam. He couldn't see what secured it on its other side.

He struggled again to see and howled as the handcuffs pared off a layer of skin. Blood trickled into his armpit. The rope remained taut.

"Finally awake?" a female voice called from behind him. Footsteps approached. Their owner slapped him on the back of the head. "Good."

She moved around Tyler. A girl in her late teens, maybe early twenties, entered his view. She wore a loose top, which failed to hide her small but athletic frame. Her blonde hair was tied back into a ponytail. She was certainly pretty and might have been a natural beauty if not for the severity that marked her features— the sharp descent of high cheek bones, the narrow bridge of her nose, the mountain peak in her eyebrows, and even the way the corners of her mouth were the only parts that seemed to smile or frown. Hers was a hard face. No doubt, a hard life had formed it.

Her sapphire-blue eyes—by far her most striking features— dazzled like disco balls, the sparkle ever moving as if responding to an unsettled mind. She was smiling, but danger lived behind that smile. Tyler didn't need to be tied up to see it. Although something about the girl was familiar, he couldn't remember having ever met her before, and yet she obviously knew him. He could only imagine how he'd wronged her. He'd wronged a lot of people. *Only one way to find out.*

"Do I know you?"

"Maybe." The girl leaned into him, inches from his face. "Maybe not." She retreated back a step. "I doubt a prick like you would remember me. But it doesn't matter. I remember you, Tyler. I know all about you. I know all about this place, too, and everything you did here."

"Here? This place? What is this place?"

"You don't remember?" The girl paced, her forefinger curled

upon her chin. "I find that hard to believe. It wasn't easy to find this place, you know? Someone on the search team must have found it and dismissed it. How they ignored those stains on the floor is beyond me. But I did my own investigation. For over two years, I searched and searched, long after those good-for-nothing cops and park rangers had given up. I wouldn't have guessed it would be so far around the lake from where..."

She wiped her eyes and swallowed down the pain. "But I found it, as you can see. Me. Alone. No one else. I didn't need their help, and I don't need it now."

"Lady, I have no idea—"

She spat in Tyler's face. Unable to wipe it off, Tyler cringed as warm phlegm slid down his cheek.

"This is where it all happened, isn't it? This is where you did it, you sick fuck."

She jabbed him in the stomach, knocking the air from his lungs. He'd had cellmates, three-hundred-pound men, who couldn't hit that hard.

The girl sneered. "I've waited a long time for this. I couldn't figure out how I was going to get you here. All those hours I spent watching you, waiting for an opening, and you just up and drive here like it was part of some divine plan. Why? Did you want to relive your glory days or something, sicko?"

Her words came out faster and faster, with more bite than a shark. The faster she talked, the faster she paced. She stomped her foot and paused, letting out a long, slow breath. "I guess I should be thankful, though. You made it so much easier for me."

"Look, miss. I don't know what you think you know, but I'm nobody. I don't have a penny. I don't have any friends or family you could blackmail. I don't even have a dog. Hell, I've been upstate for the last—"

"Six years." The girl laughed again, but this time it was downright sinister. "You poor baby. You lost a measly six years of your life, and you think that was fair?"

Tyler's walls shot up. He had been punished. In the eyes of the law, he had done his time. Sure, maybe it wasn't all that he deserved. Maybe it wasn't all he felt he deserved, but he had experienced more than his fair share of punishment over the course of his twenty-two years, more than this bitch could ever know. Who the hell was she to judge him? What harm had he ever done her?

He gritted his teeth. "Actually, I think some things were extremely unfair, miss..."

"Now, there's something we can agree on." The girl clapped and smiled a bit broader. It wasn't the smile that caught his attention, though. It was her eyes. They weren't smiling. They were deep-blue orbs with the soul-piercing sort of glare that brought back memories. He did know this girl.

Her glare, just as it had done six years ago, stripped away his resolve. His lips began to tremble. Guilt crept up on him, and before he could even think to suppress it, it had swallowed him whole. For some reason, this judgment, *her* judgment, was the only sentence that seemed proper.

"You're..." But Tyler couldn't finish the statement. He never knew her name. To him, she had always been the girl in pigtails who haunted his dreams. She had traded two pigs for a pony, but the rest of her was the same, just a bit older and a lot more volatile. Somehow, he knew that on the day his life had reached a turning point, hers had been ripped asunder. All the pain and loss he felt, she shared. All the anger he bottled, all the vengeance he sought, she yearned to exact.

The difference was that he was the target of her hate. Maybe they shared a common enemy.

Her eyes softened. "So you do remember," she said, raising an eyebrow. A frown replaced her smile. "Good. You need to remember. Otherwise, all this would be pointless."

Tyler's head dropped. She could only have one plan for him. *Justice.* It seemed right. He accepted it, though he feared what would come. He would not beg if he could help it. He would try to give her all that she wanted and pray that it would somehow make her whole again. Deep down, he knew it wouldn't. Nothing ever would.

"Get on with it," he said.

"What's the rush? You took away about fifty years of his life. I want to make sure your pain at least feels like it lasts that long."

"I hope you know what you're doing. If you were smart, you'd leave these woods now and never look back."

"I know *exactly* what I'm doing."

Tyler doubted she grasped his meaning. He didn't want to care. He'd never cared about anyone in all his years on earth. Not until her. Guilt was funny that way. If she did what she planned, she was going to have to live with guilt herself.

Stripped of any pretense, he looked deep into her blue eyes, wondering if the girl who existed before he shot her brother still hid in there somewhere. His heart ached, not for his loss or the pain that would come, but for her loss, her pain.

His sadness made his body sag and his wrists hurt that much more. She must have seen that sadness in his eyes. He doubted she would grasp its meaning.

She pulled herself against his shirt, her mouth so close to his ear that her hot breath caused his hair follicles to quiver. "I would tell you what I've got planned for you," she whispered. "But that would spoil the surprise." She came around to face him straight on, cupped her hand beneath his chin, and raised it to her eye level. Her fingernails dug into his cheeks. "Take a good look," she said, her words almost a snarl. "My name's Dakota. Dakota Coogan. And I'm the last person your sorry ass is ever going to see."

She walked behind him and out of sight. The sound of metal against metal returned.

# CHAPTER 8

"Damn it, Tyler!" Charlie pounded his fist on his desk. He folded his hands together. *Forgive me, Lord. He promised he would come back.*

For what seemed like the thousandth time, Charlie had risked his neck for a parolee who didn't deserve it. How many times had his boss and mentor warned him not to waste his time with the clientele? "Every one of them will lie to you, cheat you, try to get one up on you and, if you're not careful, some of them might even try to kill you," his mentor had told him his first day on the job. "They're losers, the whole lot of them. People don't change. Once a loser, always a loser." Charlie could hear the man laughing now.

But that sentiment fairly summed up what the world had once thought of Charles Jackson. If it hadn't been for the guidance of Father Daltry, he'd still be a loser. He had taken refuge in a church after stealing drugs from the wrong people. High, he passed out in a pew, and when he awoke the next morning, he found himself tucked into a bed. The priest had found him and given him food and shelter and a second chance. A *real* second chance, not that flimsy kind that a criminal record afforded most ex-cons.

Charlie had always believed fate had led him to Father Daltry's church that day. He'd absorbed the priest's sermons and watched himself evolve from a two-bit hood into a respectable, hardworking member of society. Strength endured in faith, even for those who took half a lifetime to find it. Charlie became the personification of rehabilitation, but there were always skeptics who judged him for his past, even now.

Still, hope was a gift. Father Daltry had given it to him.

Charlie wanted to share that hope with others who needed it.

His mentor's scowling face appeared behind his eyes, ready to express disapproval. But Charlie hadn't listened to him then and wasn't listening now. *Don't assume no one can change just because you never could. Even a pit bull raised for fighting can be tamed with a little love and kindness.*

*Okay. A lot of love and kindness.*

Charlie snapped himself from his memories. The here and now, that was important. At the moment, his mentor's cynicism seemed valid. Tyler had promised him he would return by curfew. Parole had rules, and Charlie was their enforcer. Charlie's biggest rule was easy enough to follow: report in when required. Tyler had never missed a roll call.

Until now. Worse than that, Tyler had betrayed Charlie's trust.

He ran his fingers down his face. Charlie had taken a liking to Tyler. In nineteen years on the job, he had seen hundreds of ex-cons come through his door. He had long ago learned to recognize those who regretted their crimes and wanted to start over, who would undo the past if they only could. They were men who would walk the straight and narrow even when he wasn't looking. Of course, even loyal dogs strayed sometimes. Even the best parolees, especially the younger ones, couldn't always adhere to the endless bureaucracy that governed every minute aspect of their lives. So Charlie cut them some slack.

Then there were the killers and rapists and sick, twisted souls who lacked remorse. Half of them would be back in prison after the first month, half of those remaining after the first year. Most of the rest would be dead. The handful of hopefuls who remained, guys like Charlie himself, were men worth saving.

Tyler seemed to fall squarely into that latter grouping, but Charlie had been fooled once or twice before. He had given Tyler the day, but in his greed, Tyler had taken the night along with it. *How am I supposed to overlook this?*

He cracked his knuckles then rubbed his palms together. *Lord, I will not give up on him yet.*

Charlie's devotion wasn't just for show. He saw his work as a literal fight against the Devil for every wayward soul beneath his roof. His caseload was far too big and filled with too many nasties to save them all, but for those capable of salvation, Charlie would do whatever it took to deliver it.

He stood and snatched his keys from his desk drawer. He threw on a light jacket and exited his office, locking it behind him.

"Terry," he said to the hired muscle posing as security—one of Charlie's former projects. "Mind holding down the fort? A friend of mine is having car trouble."

"No problem, boss," Terry said, a grin spreading across his face. He tipped his cap. "Give Tyler my best."

Charlie laughed. "You know me too well, I'm afraid. But don't go sounding any alarms just yet. I should be back in an hour or so. And if God is with me, Tyler will be, too."

# CHAPTER 9

Tyler screamed. By the grace of God, perhaps, he had been able to hold it back until then, but Dakota's last cut had been deep.

Dakota had seemed to be testing him at first, seeing how far she could go before it really started to hurt—or testing herself, seeing how far she could go before her nerve faltered. The switchblade had been unsteady in her hands. Her movements were unsure. The first slice barely grazed his cheek, and he winced more for her benefit than his own. He had cut himself worse shaving.

For several minutes after that first cut, she couldn't even look at Tyler. She buried her face in her trembling hands, likely second-guessing the path she had chosen.

"It's not too late to stop," Tyler whispered.

It was the wrong thing to say. Dakota's head snapped from her hands. There was no doubt in the look she gave him—just hate. Gritting her teeth, she charged at Tyler, the ice back in her eyes, her hand clutching the switchblade white-knuckle tight and driving it toward his chest.

Tyler closed his eyes and braced himself. *This is it.*

And though his eyes and mouth opened simultaneously, each hollering out his pain in its own way, Tyler was not dead. Not yet.

Dakota arched her downward strike such that when the point entered his chest, it curved sideways and dug in and back out of his flesh. The blade opened up a three-inch gash, nearly an inch deep at its hot red center. The hole in his T-shirt was much smaller. His blood had sucked it against his skin, where it acted as a kind of nonsterile bandage. Dakota had selected the wrong blade for slicing. Switchblades were meant for stabbing.

She learned quickly. After two swift jabs, Dakota poked two more small holes in him, one in his thigh, away from the femoral artery, and the other just below his shoulder as if she were trying to miss vital organs. He grunted. These wounds were minor, superficial. He raised his head and met Dakota's stare.

Madness flashed across her face, and she lunged at him. This time, she used the pointy end properly and plunged it deep into his side. The blade passed through his skin, for sure, and maybe the meat beneath. His eyes burst open upon the impact, but the lack of pain surprised him. She might have missed everything vital, but maybe not. He tried to think what organ she might have hit. Liver, kidney, spleen—he had no idea. Did it matter? He doubted he needed it anymore.

When she pulled the switchblade free from his body, Dakota wiggled it. He bit his tongue so hard that he swallowed blood. More blood poured into his waistline. He'd yelled out a barrage of curse words and almost cursed Dakota, but he'd stifled his anger before he could.

It wasn't her fault. Dakota thought her cause was righteous. Tyler could do nothing to dissuade her. He wasn't sure he wanted to.

By the time her little torture session was over, Dakota would have done him a favor. She would finally have given him the escape from his memories that he had longed for but had been too cowardly to provide himself.

As he spat out his last curse word, Tyler heard something other than his own vulgarity. *Voices?* Dakota didn't seem to hear them. She was busily scrubbing blood from her hand with a cloth as if the fluid was eating away at her flesh.

He took in the cabin and for the first time noticed that it had no windows, only a door. One way in and one way out.

Dakota stood with the knife at her hip. She moved toward Tyler, her face wrought with disgust. He could tell she didn't enjoy the torture, though it didn't stop her from advancing for another stab at him.

"Wait!" Tyler shouted.

Dakota blinked and jumped backward, obviously confused. It passed quickly. She crossed her arms. "Ready to beg? You must know nothing that you say will save you now."

"Listen." Tyler stared at the door. "Someone's outside."

She tilted her head toward the door and held her breath. "If this is some kind of trick, it won't—"

The door flew open and slammed against the wall. She turned to face it, knife arm extended.

Tyler scanned the crowd that entered. He knew them: the frat boys from the campground.

"Well, well, well," said their ringleader, the older kid with shifty eyes and nine o'clock shadow that only grew in patches. He was old enough to classify as a man, but that term didn't seem to capture his mentality. A scar ran down his cheek, similar to the one Tyler imagined he'd have if he lived long enough.

"There's a party going on in this house, and me and my boys weren't invited? That sounds downright uncool to me, un-American even. What do you think of this shit, bros?"

"I don't like it much," one of the ape twins said. Tyler couldn't tell if it was Thing One or Thing Two.

"I don't like it much either," the other twin echoed.

The frat boys piled into the room, seemingly oblivious to the weapon in Dakota's hand or the bloodied man dangling from the ceiling. One look at them, and Tyler knew they weren't his rescue party.

Shifty walked within two feet of Dakota, a twin hovering at each side as if they were bodyguards for the president's brat. Their pet, Frosh, came in after them, lugging two cases of beer. He looked exhausted. When his eyes met Tyler's, his face whitened, and he looked away.

"Now, what's a pretty girl like you doing all the way out here by yourself?" Shifty asked. Tyler's forehead crinkled. Surely, Shifty didn't think she was alone. How could he have missed Tyler strung up dead center like a side of beef in a meat locker? He coughed. Shifty just gave him a nod and returned to his conversation.

No, they were not the cavalry. They had come for Dakota.

Her body stiffened. She waved the knife in front of her.

Tyler couldn't guess how she knew these boys and the trouble they brought with them. What it meant for him was a bigger mystery. The only thing he knew for sure was that these college kids were trouble. He had seen their kind plenty of times in prison and, even before that, when he'd been on the receiving end of gang brutality. These kids were predators.

*All except the youngest one.* Tyler knew the look on Frosh's face. He'd seen that look a hundred times before, on the only prison mate who didn't deserve to be locked up just before he got his daily beat down. *Stupid kid. Wrong place. Wrong time.*

"Stay back, Mark," Dakota warned, swishing the blade through the air. "Keep your thugs back, too. I won't think twice about stabbing you." She sounded as if she meant it. Looking one of the twins dead in the eye, she yelled, "You got that?"

"Poor Dakota." Mark mimed a tear. "Always getting herself into trouble." The ape twins' low laughter resonated behind him. Frosh hung back, his face pale, his eyes averted.

Mark took a half step forward.

"You'd better stay back," Dakota warned.

"Oh, but I can't, Dakota. I never could stay away from you. And you see," he said, running a finger along his scar, "we've got ourselves some unfinished business, as they say. I owe you some payback, and by the looks of it, now is as good a time as any."

"You owe *me* payback. If you didn't have your boys backing you up, I'd kill you right now, you son of a bitch."

Mark was small, but his hand moved swiftly. The back of it hit hard across Dakota's face.

She rolled with the slap. When she straightened, blood trickled from the corner of her mouth. Something rabid seized her. She sprang at Mark, the switchblade aimed at his throat.

She might have ended him if not for the ape twins. Thing One yanked Mark backward as Thing Two clenched his hand around Dakota's wrist. He squeezed, and the blade dropped to the floor. Dakota twisted out of his grasp and slowly backed away.

Mark smiled. "I don't know what you had planned for this chump," he said, pointing at Tyler. "But I'm sure he won't mind if you put his fun on hold for a bit. Besides, you know how jealous I get when people play bondage without me."

"The cops are on their way." Dakota's voice wavered. She backed closer and closer to Tyler. "They'll be here any minute now."

Mark laughed. The twins laughed with him. "I seriously doubt that. But even if they were, they'd never believe you, not with your record and him hanging there, while me and my boys are impeccable citizens." His lip curled beneath his nostril. His eyes had the sheen of an animal's.

Dakota bumped into Tyler as she retreated. The lavender smell of her shampoo mixed with the stink of sweat and clotting blood. She stopped beside him.

"Free me," he whispered. "You need my help."

"Master," Frosh stuttered, his voice scarcely a decibel louder than the squeaking mouse's. "Um, maybe we should just leave."

"Shut it, Frosh. Boys, hold her down."

Mark and the twins advanced. Dakota turned and ran. Frosh dropped the beer and bolted out the door.

# CHAPTER 10

"Are those headlights?"

Abigail could hardly believe her eyes. They wouldn't be spending their entire night traipsing through woods after all. An access road, something wide enough to drive on, was nearby. Better still, someone was driving on it.

"Hey!" she yelled. "Over here!"

KY joined in, and for once, Abigail welcomed the sound of his voice. Side by side, they sprinted toward the vehicle, breaking their promise to stay on the trail.

Her flashlight's beam swayed as she ran. Her backpack hung heavy as if loaded with iron weights. Its straps dug into her shoulders. But all the aches and pains of a hard day dissipated under those halos of light. They were more than just electrical components. They were proof of other human life out there in the wilderness, reminders of civilization and all its comforts, and omens of a brighter future. Abigail smiled wider the closer she came to them. Finally, they'd found a way out of that hellhole.

*I am never going hiking again.*

"Ah!" KY wheezed behind her. She slowed and glanced over her shoulder. Her husband had stopped. His hands rested on his knees. "Keep going," he managed to say as he struggled for breath. "I'm fine... I'll catch up."

The vehicle, too tall to be a car, passed them, but it was moving slowly. Maybe its driver was looking for them. He had to be. The ranger had sent someone out for them, and if she didn't move, that someone would drive right on by.

"Wait!" Abigail lengthened her stride. "Stop!" She burst onto the trail only a few yards behind the vehicle—a Jeep Cherokee, she could see now, the kind the park employees had. She stood on a path less than eight feet wide and covered in shin-high grass. It hid the tracks of the SUV, swiftly covering up any reminder of human passage.

Madly waving one hand above her head, the other hand aiming her flashlight into the Jeep's rear window, she tried to flag down the driver. It worked. The Jeep stopped.

Abigail held her light on the Jeep, lowering it slightly to illuminate the words written beneath the rear window: "Kansas Department of Wildlife, Parks, and Tourism." She breathed in exhaust, marveling at how seven innocuous words could feel like salvation.

KY nearly tackled her as he tripped onto the path. He stood and dusted himself off. Mud caked his knees. His dopey smile filled his face.

*Useless.* Abigail huffed. She tapped her foot as she waited for the driver to emerge from his vehicle. At last, the driver's side door creaked open. A black-booted foot appeared, followed by olive green khakis. A tall, lanky man with a long, wiry beard and a slight potbelly exited the Jeep.

"Hiya, folks," he said, approaching. He put a hand over his eyes as if his absurdly large hat wasn't enough to shade them. "Ma'am, would you kindly refrain from shining that light in my face?"

"Sorry." Abigail shook the flashlight as if it were defective and clicked it off. The Jeep's taillights brightened the path behind it and briefly lit the man as he passed in front of them. As if the vehicle weren't proof enough, the man's garb made it clear that he was a park ranger, tried and true. His name tag read, "Merwin."

He turned toward KY, hand extended. "I take it you're the folks I spoke with earlier."

KY nodded. The ranger shook his hand.

"KY."

"You're kidding me?"

When KY stared back blankly, the ranger cleared his throat. "No? Well, I'm Merwin. Says so right here on my name tag." He pointed to over the breast pocket of his tannish-green shirt.

"Well, since you ended up on this trail, perhaps I wasn't clear on the phone. You should have taken a *left* at the fork." Merwin stared at KY then squinted as if sizing him up. "Come to think of it, I'm pretty sure I told you that."

KY shrugged and chortled. Abigail fumed silently.

Merwin presented her his hand. She took it and was surprised at the strength of grip from a skeletal waif of a man with a malnourished-looking potbelly.

"And you must be the brains of this operation," he said, smiling politely.

Abigail smiled back. Already, she liked the park ranger. The fact that he was going to get her back to her home and into a nice, warm bath placed him somewhere near Jesus Christ and Superman. She would have to remember to send him a thank-you card.

"Anyway," Merwin said, breaking several seconds of silence, at which point Abigail realized he must have been waiting for her name. "When you guys never came moseying into the station, I figured I'd better come have a look for you."

KY gave her a look, his silly grin running rampant. She met it with a look of her own that said, in no uncertain terms, to shut his hole about the ranger's use of the word *moseying*.

By the time she turned back to face Merwin, all trace of her anger had vanished. "We are extremely glad you did," she said, blushing. She elbowed KY in the side.

"Uh, yes. Thank you."

"Why didn't you introduce me?"

"Uh, this is my wife—"

"I'm Abigail. It's a pleasure to meet you."

"Delighted to make your acquaintance," Merwin said, bowing slightly. "Well, hop on in. These woods can be downright treacherous at night. I don't give a damn how much bug spray you two are wearing—and believe me, I can smell it over your stink. You are going to be scratching like mongrels tomorrow, I reckon."

"There's something to look forward to." Abigail rolled her eyes toward KY. She didn't have to belittle him again. His silence served as proof that he recognized how badly he'd screwed up.

The three walked toward the Jeep. Abigail took the passenger seat. KY sat behind her, out of sight. It was going to be a quiet ride home.

Merwin got in, dropped the emergency brake, and shoved the clutch out of neutral. The Jeep jerked forward.

"I'm just going to pull up to the lake. It's up ahead, not far. The path opens up a bit. It'll be easier to turn around. Trying to do it here is next to impossible without doing a seven-million-point turn."

Abigail's breath caught in her throat. She didn't know how to delicately word the question that was running through her mind, so she just came out with it. "Did you ever find the person who we heard screaming?"

KY scooted to the middle of the back seat. He leaned closer.

"I drove up here earlier, when you called," Merwin said. "But I didn't find anyone. I walked into the woods pretty deep, too. Didn't find anything. You probably just heard some kids fornicating. I bet they took off when I came looking. We get a lot of that out here. Weirdos who like to go *au natural*, get freaky with nature and all that jazz—"

"It sounded like someone was in pain."

Merwin tugged his beard. "Funny thing, though—I didn't see anyone in the campgrounds neither. I mean, I saw a few tents and campers, but I haven't really seen many people around today 'sides you two and one or two others. I guess they probably found a nice, secluded spot to do their thing and are getting to it. There was this young couple in one of the deeper, more private lots. I thought it might have been them who you heard. That girl had a set of bazookas that could get a dead man hard, and I ain't talking about no rigor morosis, if you catch my drift."

"Rigor mortis," Abigail corrected under her breath.

"Huh? Anyway, I couldn't find them when I checked. But their stuff's still there, and their car's still sitting in the parking lot." Merwin shook his head. "Probably some fool Yankees who don't know a thing about camping. They have a bumper sticker says, 'I brake for moose.' Ain't no moose out here."

"You don't think something could have happened to them,

do you?" KY sounded like a child scared by a campfire ghost tale. Abigail wondered how she could be legally tied to such a pussy.

"I doubt it. This shit happens all the time, believe it or not. People go into the woods and leave the trail for whatever reason. Sometimes they come back on their own. Sometimes we have to go find them."

"What if someone needs our help?"

Merwin squinted at Abigail. *Is this guy not listening to a word I'm saying?* his expression said. Abigail shook her head, embarrassed.

Merwin twisted in his seat, looking back at KY even as the car progressed forward. "Let me spell it out for you, son. There's not much we can do for them. I won't be able to find my own dick out here in the dark, let alone a lost tourist. I'll check again in the morning. It was dumb luck you two found me when you did."

The Jeep lumbered deeper into the forest. Abigail's body odor mixed with the wet-dog smell of the vehicle's interior. She cracked her window just enough to let in some fresh air and, she hoped, not too many bugs. After pulling a bottle of water from her backpack, she opened it and gulped it down. One positive thing she could say about her husband: he had come prepared for the worst. He had stocked her backpack just as completely as he had his own. As the lukewarm water cascaded down her parched throat, the extra weight she had lugged all day seemed worth it.

Merwin pulled to a stop and leaned over the steering wheel, straining to see what was in front of them. "Motherfuckers."

He huffed as he stormed out of the Jeep, arms swinging like an enraged gorilla's. Abigail watched him through the windshield as he crossed in front of the headlights. On each side of the road were two stone pylons. A rope dangled from the right pillar. Someone had snapped it off the other.

Merwin dragged the rope out of the way. The sign attached to it slid across the ground. Abigail couldn't make out what it said.

When he had removed both rope and sign from the Jeep's

path, Merwin strode back to the car, still angry. "I bet it was them damn college brats who broke it. No one respects nothing in this world."

Abigail guessed he was mad because someone had vandalized the sign. *Hardly the end of the world.* She couldn't be certain, so she remained silent. KY, fortunately, kept his big mouth shut, too. Merwin grumbled and thrust the Jeep into gear. It crawled forward into denser woods.

After about a quarter mile, Merwin threw a thumb out to his left. "The lake's over there. No one's supposed to be out this way anymore. A long time ago, when I was a boy, it was a great place to fish and swim—crystal-clear waters, nature at its most beautiful." Merwin seemed lost in a memory. He sighed. "Can't swim in the damn thing now, though. There's something rotten about it. Nothing but swamp. It gets worse every year, like whatever's polluting it keeps spreading."

"Did someone dump, like, toxic waste or something into it?" KY asked.

"Hell if I know. I've never seen anybody dumping waste, but the lake stretches out for four or five miles. I can't understand it. The water used to be the highlight of this park, full of life. Now, nothing lives there. It's like death itself bubbled up from under it and anal raped all that was clean and pure in it."

Merwin's eyes glazed over yet again. He was no doubt recalling some fine day from his youth. Abigail huffed. *Time has a funny way of destroying good memories.*

The Jeep rocked as it crept forward, the terrain beneath it uneven and overgrown. Abigail stared out Merwin's window, hoping to catch a glimpse of starlit water. Nothing could be seen but eternal blackness.

"Well," Merwin said after a few minutes of silence. "Let's get you two home. There's a small field just ahead. I can turn around—"

A loud thud came from overhead, on the roof. It sounded as if the sky had rained a pumpkin on the car. Abigail jumped, her breath catching in her throat.

Merwin nearly leapt from his seat. "What in the hell was that?" His foot slammed down the brake.

Abigail wondered if a branch might have fallen on them. On the inside, the roof maintained its normal shape, so the damage probably sounded worse than it was.

Merwin turned in his seat, looking out every window. Abigail clicked on the dome light. She saw nothing out of the ordinary, just the Jeep's hood, the trees, and darkness.

"It sounded like a coconut."

Merwin twisted in his seat, offering KY a look that wasn't short on disgust. Abigail ran her fingers down her face.

"A coconut? Do you see any palm trees out there, son? There ain't no coconuts in these parts. And this ain't no Monty Python neither. There are no sparrows of any geological origin dropping coconuts like stealth bombers from above. We only have the miniature kind, 'cept we call them *acorns.*"

Before the conversation could deteriorate further, another loud thud seized their attention. This one came from the direction of the hood. Caught up in Merwin's bickering, Abigail hadn't seen its source. Her heart pounded as she searched for the cause.

All eyes were forward. All mouths were silent. Abigail saw nothing.

Something moved on the hood. "There!" She pointed. At first she thought a puddle had formed, a buildup of water released onto the hood when the branch or whatever it was fell. The Jeep's metallic green paint seemed to spill over itself, flowing like a fresh coat applied too heavily. It spread across the hood like syrup poured onto a table, its edges creeping closer, up an incline, just beyond the range of the dome light.

Just beyond clear sight.

"Guys?" The others hadn't noticed it and weren't paying attention to her. Something about that liquid mass caused Abigail's knees to shake. She wanted to leave. She wanted to leave now.

"I didn't say it *was* a coconut. I said it sounded *like* a coconut," KY said.

"It sounded like any damn hard object falling from above and denting my goddamn roof. That's what it sounded like. Coconuts—"

"Guys!" Abigail shouted. That got their attention. They quieted again. If they hadn't seen it before, she would make them see it now.

"What is that?" KY asked, sounding both fascinated and disturbed. "It looks like a bear took a shit from a perch above us, and its loaf splatted right onto your hood."

"That ain't no turd, son. That thing's moving."

Abigail tapped on the glass. The shit pancake was moving in slow, rocking motions like the rolling and receding of the ocean. It never entered the light, as if some invisible barrier stood in its way.

With a loud pop, the Jeep tilted onto its left axle.

"Oh, for crying out loud," Merwin said, reaching for his door latch.

Abigail grabbed his forearm. "Don't go out there."

"Why not?" Merwin asked the question, but his hand retreated from the door. "I admit, I haven't a clue what that is, but there ain't nothing in these woods that has ever hurt me, except for a thorn or two. Maybe a few bee stings. And there was that possum that was playing possum, the little devil... my point is, I'm sure it's safe. Anyway, we just blew a tire, and it sure as shit ain't gonna change itself."

Scraping, like someone etching his name in concrete, came from above. "Sounds like there's another one on the roof," KY said, his eyes rolling upward. Abigail heard it, too. Whatever was up there was moving. Was it trying to get in?

The dome light shattered within its casing. The cab went dark.

Another shit pancake sprang from the darkness and hit the windshield in front of Abigail. She released Merwin's arm and huddled in her seat. Her eyes widened. She bit her thumbnail. The pancake thing liquefied before her and slid down the windshield into the crease below, disappearing beneath the hood.

"Let's just get out of here." The shit pancakes unnerved Abigail. If not for their movement, she would have dismissed them as little more than mud pies—the kind of wet, stinking filth one would find a few layers beneath the lake bed—thrown by some punks having a good laugh at their expense. That would have been a perfectly well-reasoned explanation. Merwin had mentioned something about college kids who had caused some sort of trouble. Maybe they were pulling a prank. That made more sense than the alternative.

But mud pies didn't move. At best, they might slide down a slope. The thing on the hood certainly seemed to be edging closer.

Merwin's forehead furrowed. She could tell he didn't like the look of those things any more than she did. That made Abigail's spirits sink a little deeper.

"Please..." she said.

"I can't drive with that tire like that. It'll damage the wheel, screw up the alignment—"

"We need to leave this place."

Merwin gave her a long, hard look, the fear in his eyes reflecting her own panic. "Okay. You don't have to tell me twice. Hang on, now." He stepped on the gas. The Jeep jolted forward. The headlights flickered. The engine sputtered.

"No." Merwin's mouth hung open in disbelief. The Jeep rolled to a stop. "It can't be. This baby has never given me a lick of trouble."

Abigail didn't have to say it, but she did. "I think one of those things went under the hood." Her voice was barely more than a whisper. The implication was clear. She and Merwin rolled up their windows. Abigail's got just within a crack when the battery died completely.

"There's a flashlight under your seat," Merwin said, his voice low.

Abigail listened. That scraping noise came not only from the ceiling but from under her feet as well. Slowly, Abigail reached beneath her seat.

"Ouch!"

"What is it?" KY asked. "Are you okay?"

"Yeah." Abigail sucked on her middle finger. "I just cut myself on something." A small dab of blood bubbled from her fingertip. Again, she sucked it clean.

"Probably my box cutters," Merwin said. "I have an awful tendency to leave the blade out."

Abigail sighed and reached beneath the seat, this time with more caution. She hated taking her eyes off that detestable thing that lay inches from the windshield. When she found the flashlight, she handed it to Merwin then reached into her bag for her own.

A series of thuds came from the left side of the Jeep. KY slid behind Abigail. Merwin shined his flashlight on the windows. A black bulbous mass clung to the window behind him, but it disappeared as soon as Merwin's light found it. A trail of mucus-like liquid remained where the creature had been. There was no mistaking it now. Those things weren't mud pies or shit pancakes. They were alive.

As Merwin circled the cabin with his flashlight, more thuds hit the vehicle's left side. Abigail's eyes followed Merwin's beam. She hadn't noticed the black oval, slimy and pulsating in front of her, until it had expanded itself across the windshield. Another two of those things were inches from Merwin's face. Only the thin pane of the driver's-side window separated two beings at opposite ends of the evolutionary chart. A moment earlier, that glass had not been there.

"Son," Merwin began, sounding a million times calmer than Abigail felt. "My rifle is behind you. If you'd be so kind…"

Without a word, KY reached behind himself. He grabbed the sleek steel barrel of Merwin's rifle and swung it delicately through the air so that Merwin could grab it by the stock.

Merwin took it and rested it across his lap. He put the Jeep in park and turned the key in the ignition. Nothing happened.

Abigail stared at him, wanting answers he probably couldn't give. Her whole body trembled. What was happening to them? What was going to happen?

"Just sit tight," Merwin whispered. "Maybe we should be as quiet as possible. I ain't never seen anything like this before, but as long as those things stay out there and we stay in here, we should be just fine."

"What are they?" KY was huddled so close to them he was practically in the front seat.

Merwin rubbed his forehead. "I don't know. I have a bachelor's in biology, but that's about as far as I went in school.

And that was a long time ago. They look like some sort of big, fat slug. Maybe they've been allowed to grow out here unbothered for so long that they've evolved to stave off predators. Ain't no bird gonna carry off that worm, that's for damn sure. Not even those that can carry coconuts."

"What do they want with us?" Abigail asked.

"Nothing, I bet. They're probably like bugs and were attracted to the light."

"But the lights are out."

"Listen. I think we are all getting a bit worked up over nothing. Those things are freaky-looking fuckers. I'll give you that. But they're probably harmless. I mean, who's ever heard of a person being killed by a slug? And let's not ignore the bright side: we may end up on that there Discovery Channel for finding a new species. We can name it after KY, here, on account of all the sliminess."

Merwin smiled and gave her a wink. Even KY laughed a little. Abigail began to feel better. Not good, but better. Merwin's words made more sense than anything she could come up with, and that had to count for something. She almost found them comforting.

Then she looked forward. Even without eyes, that thing on the windshield seemed to be staring at her.

Abigail slowly extended her hand toward it. A sort of morbid curiosity had caught her in its throes. The blood bubble had reformed on her fingertip. Inch by inch, her hand moved closer. Neither Merwin nor KY stirred. Neither did the thing outside. It froze as if it were watching her, waiting to strike.

When Abigail's hand was only two inches from the windshield, she felt warmth emitting from the creature. It seemed to sense her warmth, too. Its head, or maybe its tail—both ends of the creature seemed identical—peeled back from the windshield. It thickened, forming what looked like a muddy footprint on the glass. The middle of the blob thinned, the creature taking on the shape of a peanut. The tapered section slid up and down the length of the blob.

Her curiosity reverted to sheer revulsion as the creature unveiled a circular cavity where Abigail supposed its mouth might be. The mouth, if that's what it was, wasn't all that dreadful—a black hole, nothing more—but what lined it was grotesque. Thin gray appendages like squid tentacles curled and twisted in a perfect circle, rising from the depths of a black-licorice gelatin mold.

An equally revolting slurping sound came from the tentacles. It reminded Abigail of how she used to irritate her mother by sucking on a straw long after her drink was empty.

The creature revealed another of its secrets. Two rows of spines, small but talon-sharp, protruded from its body, running its full length. Its head whipped back, taking half the creature's body with it. When the thing returned a split second later, it drove its spines into the windshield. The fiberglass spiderwebbed beneath the impact.

"Time to go," Merwin said.

The little bastard recoiled for another swing, then another. Scraping came from above, below, and to Abigail's left. More creatures flung themselves against Merwin's door. Glass began to crack. Spines broke through steel and aluminum. The fuckers were trying to get in.

"Looks like the proverbial shit is about to hit the fan. I think we best be moving."

Merwin slid toward her, but Abigail wouldn't budge. She looked at him and shook her head.

More thumping. More scraping. Fiberglass crinkled like popping bubble wrap.

"Now!"

Before she could react, her door was thrown open.

KY grabbed her hand. "This way," he urged. For yet another time that day, Abigail let him lead. She reached for her backpack, but Merwin shouted for her to leave it.

"It'll only slow you down," he said, pushing her out.

Her legs ached as she found herself running. KY plowed through thick brush, blazing a trail away from the lake, away from the walking path, away from the Jeep, and away from Merwin.

*We can't leave him.* Where had KY's sense of chivalry gone? Then she realized it had never been more prominent. He was only concerned with saving her.

Abigail struggled to keep her feet. She tripped over roots and shrubs with nearly every step, barely able to see where she way going and paying little attention to it. She put her trust in KY to lead her out of hell.

Glancing back, she saw Merwin madly waving his flashlight, searching for a clear path. Everywhere its beam hit, Abigail saw those ugly slug things, screeching and moving against all the laws of gravity and inertia. They had no feet to propel themselves, no wings to fly, yet there they were, bouncing, rolling, and slinking through the brush with alarming speed— and not just one or two here and there. Abigail saw dozens of them, slurping and hissing, screaming like children on fire.

The Jeep disappeared beneath a horde of swarming black. Merwin was surrounded. There was no going back.

And there was no stopping, either. They were coming for her.

"Go!" Merwin yelled. "I'll be right behind—" His sentence ended with a cry. Abigail's heart sank.

*Don't look back, Abby,* she pleaded with herself. *Don't you dare look back.*

She could hear them all around her now, their droning alien and terrifying. The brush rattled behind her, even beside her. They were close.

KY's hand felt clammy in hers. Her grip began to slip. She held on with all her might, never wanting to let go.

But fate worked against her. Her hand slipped free. Her momentum carried her tumbling forward. She somersaulted back onto her feet but couldn't keep her balance, falling to one knee.

KY stopped and rushed to her side.

"Don't stop," she snapped, angry that he'd risk his life for her. Or was that guilt she felt? "Run, damn it!"

KY gasped. Something whizzed by Abigail's head so fast that she barely saw it. Wisps of her hair floated on a draft it left behind. Like a cannonball, another shit pancake propelled itself at KY. He saw it coming and ducked without a moment to spare. Judging by its size—much larger than the others Abigail had thus far seen—it might have taken her husband's head clean off.

The creature sailed into the trees before them. Abigail and KY veered left and ran even harder. Those awful things, those monstrosities, scurried like rodents across their path. KY booted one, and it sailed like a soccer ball into a far-off goal. Abigail sidestepped one, then another, wondering how long she could keep it up.

KY seemed to be running with a purpose beyond the obvious life-or-death stakes. He ran toward something. What did he see? What lay ahead?

A light glinted over his shoulder and was gone. Abigail wondered if she had imagined it, but it returned, again and again, each time KY's shoulder dropped.

*Is that a cabin?* The light was rectangular. It was ethereal, a fragile portal offering hope and safety shrouded by dying leaves and scraggly branches. She saw no yard between her and it—just death and worms.

Still, Abigail strained to reach it. What other hope of escape did she have? Her legs wobbled beneath her, a dull ache running through every inch of them. She had pushed them far beyond their limits, and yet, she asked more of them.

They had no more to give. Less than a hundred yards from the cabin, her legs failed her. She fell. Her hands and face slid along wet earth.

*I'm sorry, Karl. I should have been kinder.* One of those slug monsters landed on her back, tearing and gnashing.

White-hot pain seared through her muscle. The thing had latched onto her back like a wet suction cup against a glass surface. She felt something tugging at her arm and tried to pull away, but KY latched on, too. He helped her to her feet. His sheer will was enough to force her forward.

*Karl, you stupid fool. You ignorant, fat, heroic, mindless savior.* She could have kissed him then, if she hadn't been screaming.

"It's on my back," she managed between howls. "Oh God, it's burrowing into my back!"

KY, her knight, took control. He was a vision of assuredness, all confidence and machismo. Oh, how she loved him then. Without hesitating, he spun her around and seized the thing on her back.

He tugged. Abigail screamed. The creature tugged back.

Abigail hadn't thought the pain could get any worse, but there it was, setting her nerve endings afire. Her synapses shot thousands of needles into her brain, but no matter how much it hurt, her desire to have that murderous leech torn from her back won out over all others.

"Get that fucking thing off me!" she screamed.

KY obeyed. The slug monster's mouth detached with a popping sound, like a plunger returning to its normal shape after use. A gurgle rose from the creature's throat. The rest of the thing came free, taking with it a patch of Abigail's vest, her shirt beneath that, and some of her flesh. The layers had helped to minimize the damage, she thought, for the first time thankful to have been wearing them. She howled madly. *Well worth the pain, to be free of that parasite.*

She turned to see KY's hands clenched around a writhing, oozing mass. From its mouth, dark slime sputtered as if it were coughing up phlegm. Behind him, the very brush seemed to be rolling toward them. A wave of those creatures was about to crash down on them.

"Keep going," KY said, struggling with the slug monster.

The creature jerked violently in his hands. Abigail watched in horror as it fell to the ground along with several of her husband's fingers. He stared dumbfounded at the nubs, as if he couldn't understand where his fingers had gone. The creature hit the dirt and rebounded onto KY's shin, where it held fast.

KY reached for her with his mangled hand. Abigail took it, tears welling in her eyes, but as she turned to run, her hand glided across his bloodied palm. Her vision blurred. Her mind began to fog. Though faint, she swore she heard someone calling to them in the distance.

That sound was broken by the thump of a slug against skull. KY staggered forward, his arms out before him, pushing into Abigail. A creature writhed upon his head.

"Leave me," he said, his voice calm, his expression far from it. His complexion turned ashen gray. His eyelids drooped. Just before he fell to the ground, he managed one more word. "Go."

But Abigail wouldn't. She couldn't leave him after all he had done for her. She saw the head of a creature poking over the top of KY's. His fate was all but sealed. Still, she wouldn't leave him, not until one of them was dead. She had made a vow once. A nervous titter escaped her lips. *Till death do us part.*

She collapsed onto her hands and knees, hovering near KY as he twitched and screamed. Her mouth went dry. Her mind couldn't focus. She felt drunk. Something wasn't right. Had she really lost that much blood already?

KY rolled to his stomach, still fighting. Another one of those vampiric bastards clung to his back. Her husband crawled closer. She wanted to help him, to lead him to safety as he'd tried to do for her. Hands pulled her to her feet. They tugged her away.

"No," she begged, but she lacked the strength to fight.

"It's too late for him," Merwin's gruff voice said. He breathed heavily. His wire-brush beard tickled her cheek.

"Over here! Help!" another voice shouted, high-pitched but male. Abigail struggled to keep her eyes open.

"Get back inside," Merwin ordered. With his assistance, Abigail found herself standing, putting one foot in front of the other. She felt like a puppet on strings, and she began to move faster. But toward what?

"Holy shit!" A boy with curly hair came into view. "What are those things?"

Merwin urged her forward. He shouted back at the boy. "Get inside, I said. They're everywhere. Be ready to slam the door behind us. You shut it in our faces, and I swear I will come back from the grave to tear you apart."

Light washed over Abigail. She crossed a threshold.

"No!" she shouted, turning, and dove toward her husband. With all that she had left, she forced her mind to clear. Her hand caught the doorframe and held tight.

KY was still crawling toward her. He reached out to Abigail. He needed her, but several hands were holding her back.

"Come on, KY. Come on, Karl… please." She sobbed freely. "You have to make it."

"Help me with her." Merwin tried to tear her hand from the doorframe.

Still, KY came forward like a soldier crawling beneath barbed wire. Still, he reached for her.

Abigail clawed at the floor as Merwin dragged her inside. The door slammed closed, shutting out her last glimpses of KY as the creatures fell upon him. Her damp cheeks collected dust and dirt as she slid along the floor.

The room was lit, though she couldn't see more than the light itself. Her head was groggy and her vision fleeting. Darkness beat at the door to her mind. She let it in.

# CHAPTER 11

Tyler waited for Mark and Thing One to pass by him. Thing Two, a monstrous brute with thick biceps and a tree trunk for a neck, followed behind his brother. Dakota seemed like someone who could handle herself, and maybe against any one of them she could have. But against all three?

*Why help her? They won't do much worse to her than she planned to do to you.*

Tyler winced. It was his father's voice trying to reason with him. At what time had his father ever been reasonable?

*Because she doesn't deserve this*, he answered. *She's been through enough.*

Tyler ripped himself from his thoughts, feeling compelled to help a girl who meant him harm. He shimmied the handcuff's chain across the rope by pulling his right hand down much like one would stretch out a pull string on a hoodie to shorten the other. When his left hand was close enough, he grabbed the rope and pulled himself up. He raised his knee and drove his heel into Thing Two's nose.

The crunch he heard made him smile despite his pain. Thing Two staggered backward. Blood spouted from his nostrils then shot between his fingers as he tried to plug his nose. His teeth were pink rectangles outlined in dark red.

"I'm going to fuck you up for that." He sounded as if he had a cold, swallowing blood as if it were postnasal drip. Tyler's ambush had caught him off-guard, but it had only slowed him. Worse yet, it had filled him with rage.

Thing Two raised his fists. Then he charged.

Tyler had his next move all planned out. He lifted his legs to wrap them around Thing Two's neck. He was going to scissor

Thing Two's head and choke him out or snap his neck the way he'd seen someone do in an action film.

Thing Two saw Tyler's feet coming and easily deflected them. Defenseless, Tyler became a human punching bag. By the fifth blow, it occurred to him that he had not planned his attack as well as he had thought.

Still, he'd been hit worse. The Dr. Seuss reject, big as he was, hit like a little girl—until he punched Tyler in his stab wound. That hurt.

"I'll get back to you," the twin said after throwing a few more punches for good measure. "It's not like you're going anywhere." He pushed past Tyler to join the action behind him.

Tyler wished he could see what was happening. Dakota sounded like she was putting up the fight of her life. Maybe she was even fending them off. How long could she hold out?

Objects crashed against walls. Metallic things clanged against the floor. Something heavy fell against the ropes.

Tyler's arms shot up. His knuckles rapped the crossbeam, exposing the raw tissue beneath scraped-away skin. The cuffs dug deeper into his wrists. He wondered how much deeper they could cut before they tore open his veins.

The weight against the rope lessened. Tyler grimaced and began to drop. His feet landed on the ground.

"Fuck!" Mark shouted. "The whore cut me. Will one of you pin her down already? Where the hell is that worthless pledge?"

"Don't worry. I got her," one of the twins said. Tyler could hear the smile in his voice.

*Am I free?* Tyler's arms hung in front of him. He tugged the rope and found he had some slack. It gave a little, then tightened. The struggle behind him had jarred loose the other end of the rope. That gave him an idea.

Hand over hand, Tyler climbed the rope up to the crossbeam. He twisted sideways and threw his left leg over the beam, leaving plenty of space between it and the roof for him to squeeze through. Drawing up the slack behind him, he tossed it over the beam. Then he threw his right leg over and dropped to the other side.

The activity had caused more pain to his wrists and stab

wounds. He bit into his lower lip to stifle his cries. He checked his wounds. His shirt was matted against his skin, but he didn't seem to be losing too much blood.

He quietly scooped the rope into his hands. His gaze traced the length to its other end. The only bind still holding was a flimsy knot tied around the leg of a table pushed against the shack's back wall. A large wooden barrel sat beside it, the kind that might hold potatoes, wine, or moonshine. He guessed it had once sat on top of the rope.

The table had to be heavy, or his climb would have pulled it across the room, but the part that his rope was tied to looked like a gateleg. If he could pull it so it swung toward him, he figured he could tip the table, pull himself free, and leave.

Her attackers had Dakota pressed against the back wall, each twin pinning an arm. Mark was prying down her jeans, grunting and sweating like a boar in heat. Dakota writhed and cursed, kicking with her heels. None of it did her any good. Her battle was as good as lost.

*Just leave her, man. It's not your fight.*

Tyler couldn't blame that thought on his father. That was all him. Looking at the table, he knew he *should* leave her. The rusty saw, set of pliers, power drill, and assortment of cutlery hinted at the extent of agony that would have come his way. He doubted he would have remained strong like he'd promised himself. If he had begged, Dakota wouldn't have given him a second chance. If he left without helping her, she'd never have a second chance at him.

Yet after all he'd put her through, that seemed unfair. It made him feel dirty, guilty.

*She wants to torture you. She's better off here with her brother.*

Ah, there was good ol' Dad.

Defying the man, even long after he was gone, was bittersweet. Tyler's defiance mixed with guilt, duty, and honor, and each played a part in slowing his retreat, but something else drove him to Dakota's side.

Redemption. Even if it wasn't possible, he had to try.

The frat boys were after more than just Dakota's death. They wanted to do something far worse than she deserved. She was seriously twisted, and Tyler was no white knight, but he knew what it was like to live with something like that. He couldn't let it happen to her.

He yanked the rope sideways as hard as he could. The leaf of the table, heavy with tools, folded as the leg came out from under it. Tyler yanked again, and the knot slid down as the table tipped, scattering the rest of Dakota's crude weaponry across the floor. The rope came free.

Despite the noise he had made, the frat boys paid him little attention... except for the twin tower whose nose he had broken. He released Dakota's arm and came at Tyler. Blood streaked like walrus tusks in straight lines beneath his nose.

"Leave him, Bo," Mark ordered. "He's not our problem."

"But he broke my nose."

"You'll live. Get back over here and help me with her. She's a feisty one. Not like last time, huh, Dakota?" He grinned devilishly at Tyler. "Hey, bro, the door's that way. Use it."

Bo snarled and hesitated, staring down Tyler like an attack dog. Then, like a dog, he obeyed his master. He shrank back to Mark's side.

Somehow, Dakota had managed to keep Mark from sticking his filthy cock in her, but he was starting to poke and prod her with it now, the ape twins urging him on.

*Fucking college kids. All they learn in school is how to think with their dicks.* Tyler looked for Dakota's switchblade. He saw it stuck into the wall near Bo, out of reach.

His hands tightened around the rope. His jaw clenched. A feeling began to burn inside him, slowly at first.

*Fucking rapists.*

He sprang forward. In two steps, Tyler had the rope around Thing One's throat. He yanked hard.

*The bigger they are...*

Thing One's feet left the floor. He gasped for air and clawed at the rope as he crashed onto his back. Tyler followed his motion, crouching as the big man fell, keeping the noose tucked under his chin. Moving in close, he crossed the rope ends and pulled.

The twin rolled to his stomach. He tried to stand, but Tyler buried his sneaker into the space between Thing One's shoulder blades. With violent jerks, Tyler shifted his victim so that he could see the others when they came. He crouched for leverage then crossed and twisted the two lengths of rope as if he were starting a braid.

A high-pitched whine came from below him. Thing One arched back, the veins in his neck fattening, the blood having nowhere to go. His face was already plum-colored. Desperation showed in eyes bulging as if they wanted out of their sockets. Tyler couldn't help but wonder if squeezing harder would make them pop out.

The twin was going to die. Tyler was okay with that. He had no intention of letting up.

"Hold her." Mark slung Dakota at Bo, who wrapped her in a bear hug. She looked like a child in his massive arms.

Mark pulled the switchblade from the wall. "She was going to kill you!" he shouted, trembling with rage. He cracked his neck. "I don't know what's going through that damaged brain of yours, but you just made a big mistake, bro."

*Maybe*, Tyler thought, but he refused to show doubt. He watched as Mark approached. The frat boy's steps were hesitant, cautious. While Mark took his time planning his attack, his fraternity pal's life was slipping away. Already, Thing One's flopping was down to that of a fish that had been too long out of water. *Two on one is better than three on one.* Tyler didn't want to think where Dakota might weigh in.

Dakota drove the back of her head into Bo's already broken nose.

"Goddamn it!" Bo said. Blood fell in waterfalls down the cliffs of his upper lip, restaining them red. Instinct brought his hands to his face. Dakota was free. She pulled up her pants and circled Mark, a viper certain to strike.

*Two on two.* Tyler nodded at Dakota. She nodded back. *On the same side—for now.*

"Over here! Help!" The words came from outside, from Frosh maybe. Tyler heard another voice. Someone was coming.

He kept his eyes on his circling foes. Dakota chanced a look outside. Her face registered confusion. Her second glance outside became a stare.

Mark dropped his hand by his side. "Why does it look like the bushes are following them?"

Normally, Tyler wouldn't have fallen for such a juvenile trick, but unless Mark was the star of his theater class at Kansas University East, Tyler doubted he was acting. He let the rope run through his grip. Thing One coughed and wheezed beneath him. He made no attempt to rise.

"No!" a woman screeched behind him. Startled, Tyler turned. What he saw made him shudder.

The woman, around thirty, with a hurdler's legs and a homeless person's wardrobe, clung to the doorframe while an older gentleman struggled to pull her into the cabin. Tyler recognized him as the park ranger he had seen earlier.

"Help me with her," the ranger said to anyone who would listen.

Her face, drained of blood, looked skeletal, her mouth hanging open in fright, her legs kicking. Her pupils were periods on an otherwise blank page. Tyler guessed that she was higher than Mount St. Helens. Her skin was clammy, her sweat thick as chowder on her skin. Except for her flushed cheeks, she appeared to be freezing or having a seizure with spasms afflicting her entire body. The veins in her neck and temples bulged, a dark purple fluid pumping through them.

Tyler dropped the rope and ran to the ranger's side. Before he knew what was happening, he and Dakota were on opposite sides of the woman, wrenching her off the doorframe. The woman would not relent. Her eyes shook in their sockets, the pupils still dilated to the max. In some ways, she looked like any number of junkies Tyler had seen in prison, but Tyler saw that her drug was nothing like anything he'd tried or had ever wanted to.

Frosh stood behind the door, ready to close it as soon as everyone was inside. The woman's hand came free. She went limp, muttering incoherently as they dragged her along the floor. The building shook as Frosh slammed the door shut.

Mark stood frozen, his mouth gaping. Had he seen what was out there?

The ranger latched the door and threw his back against it as it rattled in its frame. He dropped a rifle at his feet. A chunk of its stock was missing. "Well, don't just stand there, you morons. Help me."

Tyler studied the ranger, wondering if the same poison affecting the woman also affected him, but when the first bang hit the door, immediately followed by a second and a third, he ran over and braced it with his shoulder. Dakota soon added her hands. Even Mark tucked his blade into his belt and came to assist.

Bo hung back, tending to his brother. Frosh took care of the woman.

A barrage of thumps hit the door and wall. The rotted wood felt as though it would break apart with every hit. Still, the pounding came harder, faster. Tyler roared as he held back the assailants. What was outside wanted in.

*They will get in.*

Not if Tyler didn't let them.

*You can't stop them.*

He knew it was true, yet he tried. He strained against wall-rattling thuds, which came one after another for what seemed like an eternity. Finally, the assault stopped. The plywood had cracked in several places, but it had held.

Tyler eased off the door. The others didn't exactly relax, but they, too, inched away.

Mark drew his blade. He pointed it at everyone and no one at once. "Somebody's got some explaining to do."

"Put the knife down, son." The park ranger didn't look like much, but his voice commanded attention. He picked up his rifle but did not point it at Mark. "We have bigger problems."

# CHAPTER 12

The woman who'd come in with the ranger lay on her back, unconscious. She moaned and thrashed in her sleep. Every now and then, her eyelids would flutter open. Sweat ran off her forehead and soaked her hair.

Frosh took off his sweatshirt, bunched it up, and placed it gently beneath her head. He used its sleeve to dry her brow. "She's hot. I'm no nurse, but her fever seems to be through the roof. We need to get her to a hospital."

Frosh, with his baby face and prepubescent body, struck Dakota as a boy who'd been playing at being a man, somehow still innocent despite his age and the company he kept.

His stare moved from face to face, waiting for a reply, searching for someone who would answer his request. No one did. Dakota looked around the room. So many people she wanted dead were in the same goddamn place at the same goddamn time. If only she had some C-4 strapped around her stomach, she'd have blown that cabin and everyone in it straight to hell.

And those things outside would have died with them, welcomed collateral damage. She suspected that everyone else had some idea of what was out there. She'd seen something, or a lot of somethings, moving toward them fast. They had swarmed the cabin like locusts, craving what hid inside. Why? How? What? She had no answers. She only knew that leaving was no longer an option.

Watching Frosh lift the sick woman's head into his lap, Dakota felt a little guilty for not helping. Still, she didn't move, as if holding still was safer.

Frosh dabbed the woman's forehead, cheeks, and neck

repeatedly with the sweatshirt that doubled as her pillow. As soon as he removed the sleeve, her head was wet again. The woman's moans became words. She was calling out the name of someone who wasn't there. *Karl*.

Dakota studied her, searching for answers. What was happening to the woman? What were those things outside? She tried to understand what cruel god would have led that woman to those woods on that particular night when all of hell seemed to be gathering there. Dakota didn't regret her reasons for being there, but some of these unlucky people—Frosh, the woman, and the ranger—had no business getting caught up in the madness that sinners like Dakota and the others had deservedly fallen into.

Despite what anyone deserved, those vile creatures had served a purpose: they had established an unspoken truce among her human companions. If it had just been her, Mark, and Tyler, though, she wondered if she'd have opened the door and let those things in.

Dakota looked at Tyler with satisfaction as her eyes fell upon his wounds. The feeling vanished when she thought about what she'd done, what she could never have imagined herself doing when Stevie was still alive. Her eyes shifted to Mark, then the twins. The one with the bloody nose still knelt beside his moaning, gasping brother, who hadn't risen since Tyler had nearly strangled him to death. Mark was nothing without his bodyguards. She wondered why they followed him. Were they just as bent as Mark was?

Mark kept his distance from Tyler and her, but Tyler didn't seem to have a problem hanging near someone who had stabbed him only minutes prior. She couldn't figure him out and really didn't give a damn. As far as Dakota was concerned, he was just another bad apple in an already spoiled bunch.

For the moment, the people in that shack had lost interest in one another. Their eyes rarely gave each other a passing glance, their attention spent on the walls and ceiling, always shifting.

Aside from the sick woman's wails, everyone was silent. Dakota caught herself holding her breath, listening. The walls reverberated with the noises made by the creatures moving on them. The gargling sound made her skin crawl.

Mark was the first to break their silence. "Will someone please tell me what the fuck is going on already?" His voice wasn't nearly as smug and confident as it had been when it was just he and his boys against her.

Dakota scoffed. She knew Mark's type—tough in a group, terrified when alone. His bravado was failing, and his true cowardly self was rising to the surface.

Not that Mark didn't have good reason to be afraid. She was scared shitless, too. Though the creatures were no longer thumping against the door, they were still crawling on the outside of the cabin.

Their activity increased at the sound of Mark's voice as if they were drawn to it. They hissed and banged, clawed at the wood. Scratching came from all four walls. The roof creaked beneath their weight. Every so often, a row of talons or teeth, or whatever those sharp bone-white protrusions were, breached the wood and retracted as though they were trying to chew their way in.

What was stopping them? The shack was so run-down that a strong gust of wind might have blown it over. Why didn't they just come in and bring the night to its inevitable conclusion? A feast the likes of which they probably had never experienced waited under a toothpick roof between popsicle-stick walls. All they had to do was take it. Neither Dakota nor anyone else there could do a damn thing to stop them. Her only hope was that she'd get to see Tyler and Mark go first.

"Anyone?" Mark pressed.

"Shut up," Dakota said, her own voice hardly a whisper. "Can't you hear them out there?"

The park ranger threw his rifle over his shoulder and moved into the center of the room. "My name is Merwin. If you couldn't tell from my uniform, I work in these here woods." He pointed at the woman lying on the floor. "That there's Abigail. She and her husband were hiking when I picked them up. We were attacked by those things outside. They dismantled my Jeep, and we ran like hell. You guys know the rest."

"Her husband?" the fallen twin asked, propping himself up on his elbows.

Merwin studied his shoes. He shook his head. It was all the answer he needed to give.

"What are they?" Mark didn't seem to give two shits about the woman or her husband. "I didn't get a good look at them, but I know they're black and about the same size as rats. Is that what they are? Are rats trying to eat us?"

"I've never seen any rats that move like that," Frosh answered.

"I wasn't asking you, pledge."

"Oh, fuck you, Mark."

"What's that, homo? Did you say something?" Mark stepped toward Frosh, puffing out his chest like some male bird displaying himself, all pomp and no stomp. The knife in his hand must have fooled him into thinking he was tough.

"Leeches... I think," Merwin said, keeping the peace by ignoring the escalating tension. "Maybe."

"That's bullshit." Mark stepped up to Merwin. He put his finger in the older gentleman's face. "I've seen leeches before. They don't grow that big, and they don't fucking chase people through the woods."

Merwin remained calm. "You're not wrong. Truth is, I have no idea what they are. I've never seen or heard of anything like them."

Dakota's gaze fell upon Merwin's rifle. Jagged, splintering wood marked the end of its stock where its butt used to be. "What happened to your gun?"

"One of those things came at me, and I swung at it. I thought I could hit the little shit right out of the park, literally. But he clung to the butt of my rifle and chewed right through it."

"If they can do that, why haven't they shredded through this place yet?"

Merwin shrugged. "Good question."

His gaze fell on Tyler. His careful scrutiny suggested more than mere curiosity. He looked as though he was trying to place Tyler. Or maybe he was just wondering who had caused the young man's wounds.

Eventually, Merwin's stare settled on the handcuffs around Tyler's wrists. He didn't ask why he wore them or who had put them on him. He just acknowledged them and moved on, as if the cuffs were exactly where they should be.

Merwin mumbled to himself as he took in the rest of the cabin. Dakota's supplies were splayed out across the floor. Most of her tools were so old and rusty that they could have easily been mistaken as some of the shack's accoutrements, but the people assembled there, bloodied and beaten, could not be mistaken for average campers.

From Bo's nostrils and the top half of his shirt, dry blood flaked like dandruff and fell to the floor each time he moved. The other twin, finally sitting up, rubbed at the inch-thick rope burn around his neck. Tyler acted as if his wounds caused him no pain, but every now and then, a grimace would reveal the truth. The night hadn't gone as Dakota had planned, but at least there were those small consolations.

She glared at Mark. His violence had not yet been repaid. She could never forget what he had done. Had he followed her there, expecting another go at it? She'd sooner die, but she'd rather see him dead first.

Merwin cleared his throat. "I don't know what kind of party you fellas were throwing. And I don't much care. Whatever bullshit you were up to needs to be put on hold until we can figure a way out of this mess."

"Easy for you to say, old man," Dakota mumbled.

Tyler crossed his arms and chuckled.

"Who put you in charge?" Mark asked, moving to within inches of the bone-thin ranger. Everything seemed to threaten the boy's manhood.

*Probably because his manhood is as small as the rest of him.*

Merwin didn't so much as flinch. "I know these woods better than any of you, and I know the way out of them blindfolded. Listen to me or don't; I don't really care. One way or another, I'm going to find help for that woman over there. She's my responsibility. The rest of you can do whatever the hell you want. But if you get in my way, I will put you down. Am I clear, son?"

Mark stared at Merwin. His face reddened, and his eyebrows slanted inward. After a moment, he backed off.

"Yeah, if you know so much about these woods," Bo said, the words muffled by blood-clotted nasal cavities and the shirt over his mouth, "how come you don't know anything about those things outside?"

Tyler came to the ranger's aid. "Those things, dipshit, are not his fault."

Bo started toward Tyler, but Mark threw out his arm to block his path. "Not now."

"What?" Bo stopped at his leader's command. "When, then? When do I get to break *his* nose?"

"We'll deal with it later," Mark hissed. Bo, a man who looked as though he could palm Mark's head like a basketball and toss him just as easily, retreated like a scolded child.

Everyone quieted. They faced Merwin. A leader had been chosen.

"Would someone like to take the handcuffs off this guy?" Merwin nodded his head toward Tyler.

He seemed surprised when Dakota stepped forward. She let out a breath, pausing before reaching into her pocket. She pulled out a small metal key. Should she let Tyler free or swallow the damn key? Months of waiting had finally given her this opportunity. How could she be sure she'd ever have another chance?

Dakota debated with herself, but in the end, she decided Merwin was right. The good of the few innocents present was more important than her need for revenge, no matter how close she had been to obtaining it. She approached Tyler. He put out his hands, but he didn't smile or gloat. Instead, he seemed worried.

*You should be worried, you son of a bitch. I have several more knives with your name on them.*

"Don't think what you did back there changes anything," she whispered into his ear. Without an ounce of delicacy, she removed the cuffs, reveling as he winced.

She looked down at his wrists. Dead white skin jutted like malformed teeth from raw pink flesh. *Too small a price for what you did.*

"My back!" Abigail cried. Dakota whipped around. The

woman's eyes were wide open. "My back! It's on fire!"

Abigail leapt to her feet. She had gone from unconscious to stark raving mad in a matter of seconds, screaming and sweating.

All eyes were on her. She stared back, her confusion and fear displayed on her face.

She ripped off her vest and clawed at her back. "It's still on me!" she shouted. Spit flew from her mouth. Her arms flailed, trying to remove what wasn't there. "Get it off! Please. It hurts. Oh God, it hurts!"

Her fingers tangled into Frosh's shirt. She stretched it at the collar. Frosh didn't fight her.

"Please! Don't just stand there. Why are you all just standing there?" Abigail howled. "Help me. Get it off me!"

The walls themselves seemed to move. Hissing and gurgling echoed into the cabin.

"Will somebody shut her the fuck up?" Mark's face twisted into a scowl. No one moved. "Fine." He huffed as though all the world's burdens were up to him alone to fix. "I'll do it."

He walked toward Abigail.

"She's just scared and in pain." Frosh stepped between them. Mark glared at the younger boy, his eyes shooting bullets. Frosh did not stand down. Instead, he dismissed Mark with a look of disgust and turned to help Abigail.

Mark pushed him. Before Frosh could turn and defend himself, Mark raised his arms to push him again.

Tyler pushed Mark first. It wasn't a hard push, but it was hard enough to get his point across. Dakota read the message clearly: *You fuck with Frosh, you fuck with Tyler.* She didn't know what to make of it.

At some point in her frenzy, Abigail had ripped her shirt off. Dakota picked it off the ground and helped Frosh get Abigail's hysterics under control. The woman danced around in her bra and jeans, insisting that one of those creatures was tearing apart her back. She spun, and Dakota caught a full view of the cause of Abigail's distress.

To the right of her spine, midway down her back, two rows of what Dakota could only describe as holes ran down to her waistline. They oozed a slimy black fluid. The skin around each puncture was black as well, like the charred remains of a fire. Bluish-black striations, like tiny rivers with infinite branches, coursed from the wounds.

Dakota had thought she had a strong stomach—it had held up as she did things she had only previously imagined herself doing—but seeing those wounds was trying her guts. She refused to cover her mouth, not wanting to show her enemies her weakness.

Even so, something about the way those gaping dime-sized holes bubbled out their viscous black bile struck her as perverse, maybe even unholy. The smell that wafted from them, like that of a burst anal cyst, antagonized a stomach verging on eruption.

Most of the others kept their distance. Mark had withdrawn and now stood with the twins. Tyler ground his teeth, his face pale. Even Merwin covered his nose.

But not Frosh. The skinny little kid put them all to shame. He took Abigail in his arms and gave shelter to her shivering body. He showed no sign of fear, no hint of revulsion.

"It's off," he said softly as though trying to dissuade a snarling dog from biting. "You're hurt bad. You have some nasty wounds on your back, and that's probably what you're feeling. But whatever was on you, it's gone now. I promise you that."

Abigail collapsed against his shoulder. The pain seemed to have drained her. Her voice fell to a hush. "It hurts so bad," she said, moaning. Tears fell from her eyes. She rocked on her feet then dropped back into Frosh, who caught her in his arms. Tyler ran to his aid. Together, they gently lowered Abigail to the floor.

"We need to wash out those wounds," Merwin said. "Does anyone have any water? All of my supplies, and that includes my first aid kit, are back in the Jeep. So unless someone wants to volunteer to go and get them, we'll have to make do with what we have on hand."

Dakota walked to the back of the room. She paused to look at all the weapons lying on the ground. She snagged a survival knife and slid it blade first into her back pocket, wondering if the weapon would have to live up to its name. The others were watching her, but she'd have been crazy not to pick one up while she had the chance.

She lifted the table that had tipped when Mark and the twins had attacked her. A duffle bag sat behind it. She pulled a bottle of water out through its open zipper. After a moment's thought, she shuffled back through the duffle bag for another item that she had brought to prolong Tyler's life and his pain: gauze. Abigail would need it. She couldn't very well deny Tyler a piece of it without drawing the ranger's suspicion. She pulled it out and tossed it to Tyler, regretting that she was prolonging his life for reasons other than she'd intended.

He nodded his appreciation. Dakota frowned and looked away. While Merwin and Frosh sat Abigail up, Dakota carried over the water bottle. Tyler wrapped the gauze around his abdomen. He tore it off and brought the remainder to Merwin.

"Good. Thank you." Merwin opened the water and handed it back to Dakota. "Now, pour it on those wounds."

Dakota emptied half the bottle down Abigail's back. The black ooze washed away. Frosh dabbed her dry with his sweatshirt. When he was done, her back began to ooze shit sauce all over again.

"What's happening to her?"

"Necrosis, if I had to guess." Merwin said. "I've only seen something like that happen from certain kinds of spider bites. The skin literally rots away around the bite."

"Will she die?"

Merwin shook his head. "She should be fine, even if it is necrosis, so long as the rotting doesn't continue to spread. Sure, she'll have a few scars to remind her, but that's about it."

"Or she could be dying as we speak, for all you know," the rope-burned twin blurted.

Dakota didn't find his negativity the least bit helpful, though she was fairly sure the mongoloid was just stating what the rest of them were thinking.

"Yeah, you said you've never even seen those things before," his brother added. "How could you know what they can do?"

Merwin stood tall. "I can't, and I don't. So why don't we

all just work together to make sure no one else gets... bitten or whatever. You got a name, son?"

"Bo, and that's my twin brother, Luc."

Despite the direness of their circumstances, or perhaps because of it, Merwin couldn't help but laugh. Dakota saw him trying to hold it back, but he failed miserably. She couldn't figure out what was so funny.

"Really? Bo and Luc?" the ranger said.

"Yeah, our father was a big fan of—"

"Oh no, I get it. It's just terrible what parents will put their kids through."

"You would know, Merwin."

The ranger stopped laughing. He composed himself. "Fair enough. How's your nose?"

"I'll live," Bo said.

"Anyone else here got any injury that needs tending?"

Dakota looked around. She saw some heads shaking and heard some mumbling, but all things considered, the group seemed to be holding up fine.

Merwin clapped his hands. "Okay, then. Now, let's talk about how we're going to get out of here."

# CHAPTER 13

Charlie had called one of his contacts at the Cherokee County Sheriff's Office to find out if any vehicles had been reported stolen earlier that day. He was given the makes and models of two automobiles—a black Nissan Maxima and a red Honda Civic. He took down their license plate numbers for good measure. Tyler hadn't told him exactly how he planned to get to the park, and Charlie had purposely not asked, but he wasn't an idiot. He knew all about Tyler's past. At least if he saw one of the stolen vehicles at Galveston State Park, he would know Tyler was still there.

*And what are you going to do with him when you find him?*

Charlie didn't have an answer. He shook his head. If Tyler had stolen a car, his transgressions would become that much harder to ignore. Charlie was having a hard enough time looking past them already.

As he pulled into the parking lot, he immediately spotted the Honda Civic. After comparing its license plate number to that in his notepad, Charlie took a deep breath. He was happy to have found Tyler before he would have to report him for violating parole. But a stolen car? That was going to be harder to let slide.

*Maybe we can call it "borrowed."*

He parked his car beside the Honda and got out. There were few other cars in the almost empty lot. The air was still, the forest silent as if time had stopped.

*Where is everybody? It's still early in the season, I suppose.*

Technically, the park was closed, though the campgrounds farther in were always open. Since the state of Kansas couldn't exactly prohibit people from leaving, the west gate was open twenty-four seven. At night, it was the only way in and out of the park unless Charlie wanted to do some off-roading. He had used it hundreds of times to pick up clients who were judicially inspired to perform community service. The closing time just meant that it was unlikely a ranger would be there to help him.

The light shining through the ranger station's windows raised his hopes. This night was going to be different. He strode toward the structure at the end of the parking area. Once there, he knocked on the door and waited patiently.

No one came. He knocked again. He listened for footsteps or any other sounds within but heard none. The blinds on the nearby window were open. Charlie peeked into the building. The lights were on, but nobody was home.

*Unless they're hiding.* Charlie smiled. *Maybe I scared everyone away.*

His smile flipped. He needed to find Tyler before anyone else did. If the young man was caught with a stolen car, he'd be thrown back in prison as a fast as the judge could swing his gavel.

*Looks like it's time for some off-roading after all. In my Malibu.* Charlie laughed and slapped imaginary dust from his hands. He jogged back to his car. *I can't believe I'm doing this. Tyler, my friend, you are going to owe me big-time.*

He headed into the campgrounds as slowly as an old man with a walker and a busted hip. The Malibu's high beams illuminated the path, but the light ended at the heavy forest on both sides. The sky was dark, the moon and stars hidden behind clouds. He felt as if he were entering a tunnel with only a mining helmet to guide him.

Like the parking lot, the forest was eerily quiet. Where were the owls' hoots? The crickets' chirps? With his window down, Charlie could only hear the sputtering of his antique engine. He figured it would survive the trip. It was his tires that worried him.

He slapped the back of his neck. Blood and insect wings stained his palm. He found it strangely reassuring that even though he couldn't hear them, a few bugs were still present. Charlie just wished they weren't the kind that caused welts and itching.

When he reached the first camping area, he flashed his headlights at the tent he found there. "Tyler," he shouted. His watch read 11:17 p.m. "Tyler," he called again. He hated having to disturb sleeping campers, but if Tyler was in that tent, Charlie needed to know.

He got out of his car and approached the tent, leaving his headlights shining on it. "Tyler? You in there?" No one responded. "Hello? Anybody home?"

He walked slowly, not knowing who might be in the tent or what they might be doing in it. Given the total silence, he guessed they were sleeping. Hadn't he been loud enough to wake them?

*My loud mouth could wake the dead.*

He flicked the tent, not knowing how else to knock. "Hello? I'm sorry to bother you, but it's sort of an emergency. I'm looking for someone. I just want to talk to you for a second."

Still, Charlie received no answer. He thought about opening the zipper but decided against it. Invading the privacy of others didn't sit well with him. He was about to give in when he noticed a tear in the tent.

*You can't do that,* he told himself even as he crooked his neck for a better view. *As long as you don't open it with your hands, it's not really peeping.* Whatever he could see by positioning himself just right was fair game. They were on public land, after all, a place where children weren't only allowed but expected.

His logic didn't make him feel any less of a pervert. Working with Tyler was helping Charlie add new material for his next confession.

It was all for nothing. Unless a person no bigger than a garden gnome was hiding in a corner, the tent was empty. Charlie wondered where they could have gone.

He examined the tear. *That's a great way to get eaten alive.* He slapped his arm, not sure if the bugs he felt crawling over him were real or imagined.

He got back into his car and drove to the next clearing. In it, he found a Winnebago parked next to a dwindling fire. Aluminum crunched beneath his foot as he stepped out of his vehicle to investigate. A beer can curled around to his shoe. A few dozen more littered the camping area.

For the first time, he hoped he wouldn't find Tyler, at least not in that camper. Adding "passed out drunk" to the boy's list of indiscretions would not be a step in the right direction. Charlie hesitated, preparing himself for the worst, then knocked on the Winnebago's door.

No one answered. His patience started to fail him. He knocked again, loudly. *Cheese and crackers! What's going on? Where the heck is everybody?*

"Fudge it," he muttered and tried the latch on the door. It was unlocked. He opened the door and went inside.

"Aw, come on!" Charlie covered his nose with the crook of his elbow. The camper's interior was filthy. It reeked of vomit. Pizza boxes were strewn about the floor and atop the sofa bed and counter. More beer cans had been tossed into random piles or stacked in towering tributes to alcoholism.

The camper had certainly been lived in, but its residents were absent.

Charlie stepped outside. He slammed the door shut, the anger of his youth rearing its ugly head. The sound of beer cans tumbling came from inside. His outburst embarrassed him. He took several deep breaths, slowing his heart and cleansing his mind.

Then he stood silent. He listened for clues, any indicator of where society had retreated. At that point, Charlie would have been happy to find any human at all, never mind Tyler. The campgrounds were as quiet as a cemetery. The atmosphere felt nearly as bleak. For whatever reason, he was getting some seriously gloomy vibes from the place, as if God were trying to tell him to get the heck out.

*Tyler, you are going to be in a heap of trouble if you don't have a darn good explanation for this.*

He took a step. Another beer can crunched beneath his foot. A mosquito bit his neck. "Fudge!" He almost said the other F-word. Charlie slapped the bug and stared down at the can. It was flat at one end. He kicked the other end, and the can sailed into the Winnebago.

Anxiety replaced fury. *That's not good*, he thought, for the first time noticing the camper's flat tires. The vibe frequency lowered from gloomy to downright bleak. His moral compass commanded him to find his ward, to guide him from this desolate place. But that inner compass's point was also spiraling madly, unclear as to which of them was really in trouble.

Charlie hurried to the next lot. He no longer cared about respecting privacy or being polite. His mind told him he was being unreasonable, but it was his gut that he trusted, and it warned him of danger. But from whom or what?

*What have you gotten yourself into?* Charlie meant the question for Tyler, but by the time he finished the thought, he wasn't sure if he was asking himself instead.

*They're all probably just partying deeper in the woods. Maybe they took a late-night swim.* Charlie's gut wasn't buying it.

Finding the third and fourth lots empty, he drove deeper into the forest. His car squeaked like loose box springs as it bounced down the trail. After a couple of minutes, he came to a smaller lot, its opening almost entirely blocked by overhanging branches. Charlie had nearly passed it. The entrance was dark like an open mouth.

He angled his Malibu to shine as much light as he could inside the camping area. He dared not drive the car in for fear he wouldn't be able to drive it back out. A tent sat on the far side of the lot. Charlie hustled toward it, calling Tyler's name.

He didn't announce himself again before unzipping the tent flap. Somehow, he knew he wouldn't find anyone inside. He was right.

As his hand reached the bottom of the zipper, it brushed against something wet. It painted his fingers dark. He wiped them on his pants.

*Tyler, where are you?*

Charlie considered leaving. He had already done more for Tyler than anyone else in his profession would have. He had probably done a whole lot more than Tyler's friends or family would have.

He sighed. Tyler didn't have any friends. He didn't have any family, either. He had Charlie.

How would he find Tyler? For all he knew, his charge was

long gone. Maybe he didn't come back to the house because he didn't want to come back. Charlie couldn't force him to, but Tyler's failure to report in when scheduled was a violation of his parole. Maybe Tyler was one of the lost causes after all. But what if he hadn't returned because he couldn't?

*Just a little farther in. Just in case.*

In case of what? Try as he might, Charlie couldn't conceive of the kind of trouble Tyler could get himself into out there. *The last time he was in these woods, he shot somebody.*

Charlie laughed uneasily. *You're being foolish. He's a different man.* No matter what he told himself, though, Charlie could not shake his feeling of dread.

He drove up to two stone markers, one on each side of the trail. A rope lay near the right one. Charlie assumed it had once blocked the path. Someone had been through there.

He had only traveled a few more yards when he slammed on the brakes. A family of deer sprang onto the path and vanished—all except their smallest. The Malibu clipped its leg in midflight, and it fell.

*Great. Now I've killed Bambi.* He hopped out of his car to check on the animal and inspect the damage. As slowly as he'd been traveling, he might have only knocked it off-balance. He hadn't heard a crunch or a snap.

The deer was small, probably only a fawn. It lay on its side, its stomach contracting and expanding as it took short, quick breaths. Otherwise, it remained still. Its big brown eyes watched Charlie as he approached. The animal looked terrified, but it made no attempt to flee.

*It must be hurt.* Charlie looked the deer over and squatted beside it. He could see the upper half of its body, from its nose to its tail and most of its belly, illuminated by his headlights. The belly was so fat and round that Charlie would have thought the deer pregnant had it not appeared to be so young.

He peered into the shadows, scanning what he could make out of the deer's legs. No bones seemed broken. A sort of wildness twinkled from its dark pupils, yet they were soft, gentle. They gleamed in the light, wide with fear.

"Now I know why they call them *doe eyes*." Charlie spoke softly, trying to put the creature at ease. He made no sudden movements. The deer's panic seemed neither soothed nor accelerated by Charlie's presence.

Slowly, cautiously, he reached out to touch the animal. He knew he shouldn't. It could have been sick or carrying germs or worse. *They call them "deer ticks" for a reason.* Still, those parts of human nature that made one want to pet the soft and fluffy as well as comfort the afflicted compelled Charlie's hand forward.

The deer let out a low whimper when Charlie's hand found its side. It stayed put as Charlie gently stroked it. He wondered if he was doing anything to relax the creature.

"Think you can walk? Your legs seem okay." Charlie continued to pet the deer. "Maybe if I just back away, you'll—Jesus!"

Charlie's hand recoiled. He laughed at his jumpiness. "You *are* pregnant, you little hussy." The baby had kicked right where Charlie had been petting.

"No wonder you can't walk. That thing's about ready to pop." He stared at the deer's belly, fascinated. The baby had awakened, and it was moving.

A lot.

"That fawn's coming out, isn't he?"

The deer's stomach bulged and receded. "He's kicking like crazy. I think you're going to be a mommy soon… really soon."

Charlie wondered how he might move the deer. It lay in the middle of the trail. There was no safe way around it. He returned his hand to the deer's belly. A wave of compassion washed over him. This deer needed his help. God had made all life on the planet, and that made all life important. After hitting the poor thing, the least he could do was make sure that it gave birth safely and didn't get run over. Like Tyler, that deer had become his responsibility.

"Fuck!" Something stabbed his hand. He pulled it away, asking God to forgive his vulgarity.

A small black hole dotted his palm. It looked as though he'd been stabbed by a pen and the ink had emptied into the wound.

His blood mixed with a black, oily fluid. It spilled from the cavity, streaking across his hand.

The deer convulsed. Charlie stood. He took two steps back. He didn't know what was happening, but he no longer thought the deer was pregnant. At the least, it wasn't carrying anything natural. As its stomach ripped open from the inside, Charlie had the most peculiar thought.

*Babies don't usually eat their way out of their mothers' stomachs.*

His favorite film, *Alien*, came to mind. He hurried backward to his car.

The sound of flesh ripping was joined by an unearthly wail, a shrieking hornlike noise that couldn't possibly have come from an animal's throat, yet there it was. It stopped Charlie in his tracks. A slit had formed in the beast's underside. Something was coming out of it.

He knew it was foolhardy to stay any longer, yet that black oozing mass wriggling itself free of the deer's twitching body captured his attention. Charlie could no more look away than he could walk on water. Covered in what might have been the deer's blood, the dim lighting making it appear black, a fat, worming mass emerged from the animal's belly. It resembled an organ, perhaps the deer's stomach or liver—but why would it be moving?

The mass folded on top of itself. Charlie would have believed it was looking at him, but there were no eyes. A dark cavity formed at its center. It was the size of a human eye but black and abysmal. When tendrils curling like fishhooks sprouted around it, Charlie had seen enough.

He pulled open his car door. Before he entered, he turned for one last look at the vile thing that had murdered God's good creature. He turned just in time to see it coming.

Before Charlie could react, the slimy membrane had latched itself to his face. He screamed, his mouth opening wide to bellow out his agony. He wrestled with the creature but could not pull it free. It embedded itself in his forehead. Blurry spines thrashed before his eyes, a sliver of space separating them from certain blindness. His cheeks burned with acid heat. Then his mouth—*Oh God, the thing is trying to get into my mouth!*

He tried to close it but was too late. His teeth bit into what felt like a water balloon covered in mashed banana. Its goop was secreted over his lips and onto his tongue. It smelled foul and tasted worse, with a burn like wasabi and a texture and flavor like warm, spoiled yogurt.

Charlie tried to bite down, to kill it with the only weapons at his disposal, but the creature was too thick.

It shimmied its way deeper, working slowly down his throat. Charlie gagged upon it. His lungs ached for air. His mouth tried to suck in oxygen around the creature, but instead, it only sucked the vile thing in farther.

He fell against the side of his car. With all his might, Charlie yanked at the worm's tail. He would pull it out even if he had to pull out his tongue with it.

Or he'd die trying.

# CHAPTER 14

"The noise… they've stopped."

Tyler listened. Dakota was right. If the creatures were still outside, they were taking a break, hiding maybe, waiting. He didn't like them scratching at the walls. He didn't like them silent either.

"Do you think they're gone?" Dakota asked no one in particular.

"Why don't you go check?" Mark grinned. His incisor bit into his lower lip.

Dakota stormed over to him. "Why don't you? A dirtbag like you would probably find himself in good company."

*Not a very impressive comeback.*

Mark didn't even flinch. He chuckled, evidently enjoying his ability to get under her skin. Whatever history existed between them, Tyler didn't know or care. It suited him to have Dakota's wrath momentarily redirected, though their bickering helped no one—and it was noisy. If the creatures had left, the last thing Tyler wanted was for some loud conversation to draw them back.

*You know they'll be back,* his father's voice chided. *None of your new friends are getting out of here alive.*

"Enough." Merwin's command summoned his attention. The ranger sounded like a real father should when disciplining his naughty children. Tyler nodded his agreement even though he hadn't been part of the confrontation. Dakota crossed her arms and pressed her lips shut. Mark just laughed, but he didn't fool Tyler with his tough-guy act.

*They won't last the night.*

"Well, the bitch is right about one thing," Mark said. "One of us should check if the coast is clear."

Tyler was quick to note that Mark had not volunteered. Tyler didn't volunteer either. Where was the sense in it? Whoever went out there was dead, plain and simple. Maybe the slug things would attack the first person to step outside, or maybe they'd wait until more followed. Either way, dead was dead.

*They're dead anyway. It doesn't matter if it happens outside or inside.* How Tyler wished his father would shut the hell up. He was wrong. He had to be. For whatever reason, the creatures weren't coming into the shack. As long as the slug-leech purple people eaters stayed outside and the humans stayed inside, the humans stayed safe. Why upset the balance?

Dakota surprised him. "I'll do it." She headed toward the door.

Tyler started to move, but Merwin already blocked her path. "I wouldn't. Those things… they aren't natural. It's probably best we wait out the night."

Dakota set her jaw, grumbled, "Cowards," and followed it with a few muttered curses. The hate flamed in her eyes again, but at least this time, it seemed directed at everyone in the cabin, not just Tyler.

He chuckled. *A room full of men, and she's the only one who has any balls.*

Dakota shoved her way past Merwin. Tyler followed her movements as if watching a silent film in slow motion. She reached for the doorknob. Spots of silver shimmered across a field of rust. Their twinkling glimmer had her in a tractor beam. The knob disappeared into her hand. She turned her wrist.

"Don't open it!" Abigail cried from the floor, scaring the shit out of Tyler. He wasn't the only person to jump. Her eyes had lost their haziness. Her skin remained pale, but the purple rivers under it had receded.

"If you do, you'll die."

Dakota stopped. Her head hung low. For a moment, she just stood there. Then her hand released the doorknob. She returned to the group, shuffling through a walk of shame.

Tyler offered her a friendly smile as she passed. It didn't matter that she wanted him dead. Dakota was still braver than the rest of them. That merited some recognition.

With her gaze cast upon the floor, Dakota didn't see him. Tyler was glad for it. She probably would have thought he was mocking her.

"This is bullshit," Mark said, shoving past Dakota toward the door. "They're gone." He laughed, but anxiety, not mirth, fleshed out the sound of it.

"They're waiting," Abigail said flatly. Maybe it was her matter-of-fact tone. Maybe it was the dire certainty in her voice. Her words made Mark shrivel like genitals in icy water. He froze then dropped his hand from the doorknob.

"How could you know that?" he asked, his voice high-pitched and wild. "How could you possibly know that? They're just animals. Stupid, mindless animals."

"Kind of like you?" Dakota asked.

Abigail fixed her stare on Mark in a way that seemed to hypnotize him. He didn't take Dakota's bait. The injured woman sat up as straight her damaged flesh would allow. "I know because I... I can *feel* them. I can feel their hunger. They're in my head. I can *see* them."

"She's hallucinating. That thing must have poisoned her good," Mark said.

"Maybe," Merwin answered. "But she seems pretty lucid now." He took Abigail gently by her arm. "What is it, Abigail? Do you know something about these creatures? What do you see?"

Her eyes rolled up into her head, exposing blank white sheets. "Death. Piles of bones picked clean. Human bones. Our bones. This is what it wants. This is how it lives."

Abigail's eyelids fluttered. Tyler couldn't tell if she was conscious or not or how she remained standing.

"It?" Merwin asked. "Not they?"

"She's lost it, man." Mark huffed. "Look," he said, waving his hand in front of Abigail's face. Abigail didn't flinch. "Nothing. The girl's gone. Am I the only one who sees this?"

"He may be right, Merwin," Frosh added. "She's feverish. That thing did a number on her. Who knows how its poisons worked on her mind?"

Though Abigail had spoken her words clearly enough, Tyler

could see that their meaning had been lost on the majority of the people in the cabin. *They're afraid,* his father's voice whispered. *They should be.*

"Finally, someone else with some sense." Mark shot the twins a dirty look as if to ask them why they hadn't backed him up.

Abigail's eyes returned to normal. Her emerald-green irises shimmered with confusion. "Where am I? Who are you?" She crossed her arms over her chest. "Where are my clothes?"

Frosh approached with caution. For whatever reason, he had taken on the role of Abigail's caregiver. "You were bitten by one of those slug things. This man carried you in here. He saved your life."

Abigail faced the park ranger. "Merwin? I remember. Karl... he fell. He didn't make it?"

Merwin made an attempt to answer, but he choked up and looked away.

Abigail's eyes filled with tears. Then, as if her body just remembered its hurt, she gasped. "My back," she cried, twisting to look over her shoulder. "It burns. Is that monster still on it?"

*Monster?* To think those black slimy slug things were some long-lost relative of a leech was quite a stretch. But monsters were the creations of books and movies. In the real world, men were the only monsters.

"Not this again," Mark said, rolling his eyes.

Frosh put out a hand to silence him. Amazingly, it worked. "No, it's gone," he said, handing Abigail her shirt. A long strip was missing from its back. He gave her his sweatshirt as well, smiling weakly. "I promise."

"I can still feel it, sucking and tearing, like it's trying to get inside me."

"It got you pretty good, but you seem to be getting better. We were all worried for a while there."

Tyler and some of the others mumbled their agreement. The truth was probably that only Frosh and Merwin were genuinely interested in the woman's welfare. Mark didn't even bother to fake it.

"Speak for yourself," he said.

Frosh balled up his fist. "Do you ever have anything useful to add?"

"What's it to you?"

He came at Frosh, but it was Abigail who reacted. She kneed Mark in the balls so hard that they might have found a new home in his stomach. He bent at his knees, grunting in pain and anger. He pulled the knife from his belt.

"Don't," was all Merwin said. It was enough when combined with the hand he tapped against his rifle.

Mark moved into the corner. "You said they were still out there." He spat. "I want to know how you know that."

"I don't—"

"Bullshit. How can you feel them? How can you see them? What the hell did they infect you with? Maybe we should just throw your whore ass out there and see what comes a-knocking."

"Why do you always have to be such an asshole?" Dakota twirled the point of her blade on her fingertip. Tyler hadn't noticed her draw it. He'd have to start paying more attention to those sorts of things if he wanted to live—and for some reason, he did. Maybe the prospect of being eaten alive had cured him of his suicidal tendencies.

*I need a weapon.* He sighed. *As if I don't have enough to worry about.*

"I'm not going out there," Abigail stammered. "I'm never going out there."

"No one is." Merwin turned to Mark. "Unless you want to go yourself?"

Mark shied away. He looked as though he were going to explode.

*Used to getting your way? What a spoiled rich kid.* Tyler doubted that Mark was capable of ever being anything more.

Distracted by his thoughts, Tyler didn't notice Merwin approaching until he was right in front of him. Dakota stood beside Tyler, still twirling her knife on her finger. Frosh was busy filling in Abigail on all that had happened since she fell in the woods. Abigail listened as she dressed. One of her sneakers was missing.

Mark hung back, whispering with the twins.

"Look," Merwin said, meeting Tyler in the eye. "I know who you are, and I can pretty much guess who she is." He pointed at Dakota. "I've been working these woods here since before the ill-begotten loads that produced you two were spent. Tyler Kendrick, your face was plastered all over every newspaper and television station in the state when you shot that Coogan boy. Hell, I was working the day you did it."

Out of the corner of his eye, Tyler saw Dakota tighten, her jaw and hands clenching. Tyler tightened in response. He offered no admission or denial.

Merwin looked Tyler up and down. "Yeah, you're older now. I didn't quite place you right away. But I remember now."

Tyler wasn't sure where the park ranger was going with the conversation. His muscles tensed, ready to act if they needed to. Merwin was Tyler's best bet at finding an ally among those present. Who else would there be? Abigail? The kid maybe? His pickings were slim.

Though he kept his anxiety hidden, Tyler squirmed beneath Merwin's gaze. The memory of that day had haunted him enough, and in the last twelve hours, it hadn't stopped haunting him. He flexed his fingers and bounced on his feet. Only an old man and a girl stood between him and the door—an old man with a rifle and a girl who had taken on three attackers at once. If he made it by them, would he be leaping out of that infamous frying pan?

Merwin came no closer. "The Coogan boy had a sister. I couldn't remember her name until I heard yours, Dakota. Ain't too many Dakotas running around, I figure, least not with a hard-on for Tyler here. Given that he was all handcuffed and cut up, this place littered with more cutting utensils than a Swiss army knife, I'm guessing you were just getting started on some good old-fashioned revenge."

Dakota gaped, speechless. Tyler kept his poker face, neither confirming nor denying Merwin's assessment. He awaited the old man's next move.

"He killed my brother." Dakota's voice came out low and growling.

Tyler could keep silent no longer. "I *shot* your brother. I did not *kill* him. At least, I didn't want to, but I've been living trapped in that single second, when my finger squeezed the trigger and your brother fell, for the last six years of my life."

"Aw. Do you expect me to feel sorry for you?" Dakota stopped twirling the knife. She raised its point toward Tyler. Merwin grabbed her wrist softly but firmly.

"I remember the events of that day perhaps as well as the two of you. Three people went missing. Only your brother came out of those woods. The day he died was the first of many I spent searching for his friends. They were never found, not by me, not by no one. In all likelihood, they're still in these woods, dead and buried… or digested."

"I bet you *he* knows where they are." Dakota tapped the flat side of her blade against Tyler's chest. The anger and hate in her eyes had returned. If she so chose, not even Merwin could stop her from killing him then.

Merwin raised his hands in front of him. "But here's the thing. Your brother's friends weren't the first to go missing in these parts, and they weren't the last, neither. Now, I'm not excusing anything Tyler has done, but I saw your brother that day. And I've seen what those things outside can do—what they did do to that poor woman's husband."

The three of them looked at Abigail. She was out of earshot, still talking with Frosh.

Merwin took a deep breath. "I'm not saying he didn't kill your brother, and I'm not saying he did. But I'm guessing those creepy critters didn't just spring into existence overnight. I'm guessing they've played a part in some, maybe most, of the disappearances. I have no proof of that, of course, but—"

"No," Dakota said, crossing her arms. "You don't."

"Be that as it may, I had thought you two were going to be the glue that held this group together, so to speak. Whether you believe me or not, the way I see it, we have to stick together. We have to stay strong. And we may have to fight… them, not each other. From what I've seen, Abigail is a lot tougher than she looks, but man, the shit she must be going through in her head right now. And who knows how that creature's juicy juices are messing with her brain."

He pointed at Frosh. "That boy seems like a good egg, too, but soft. Hard to say where his loyalty will lie when push comes to shove. And those other three? Shit, you'd have to be blind not to see what they're made of. Wolves in frat boy clothing."

Tyler couldn't argue with that, though he thought Merwin was too optimistic if he expected Dakota to put aside her murderous intent, even for just a little while.

"So that leaves you, me—"

"And the Devil makes three?" Dakota cast Tyler yet another hostile look.

"Something like that. Come on! Neither of you wants to be worm food any more than I do. We'll have an eternity for that after we've lived long and hopefully happy lives. Our best chance of getting out of here is by working together. You know, strength in numbers and all that bullshit. All I'm asking is that you two table your differences for now and help me get this group to safety. Can you do that?"

*Yes, Tyler. Help lead them to safety.*

Tyler nodded, choosing to ignore the voice in his head. He'd never wanted to harm Dakota. If he had known she would follow him there, he'd have kept miles away. But whether she agreed with Merwin or not, Tyler knew better than to trust her.

Her arm relaxed. Merwin released it and took a step back, studying her closely.

"Okay," she whispered. "For now."

"Guys," Frosh called. "I've found something."

# CHAPTER 15

Dakota was wondering how the night had gotten so fucked-up. It was supposed to consist of her, her brother's murderer, and payback for a wound that would never heal. She had stabbed Tyler deep—at least she thought it had been deep—but the son of a bitch showed no signs that it even affected him. His shirt still looked damp where she had sliced through it, though. With any luck, he'd bleed out before the night was over.

*No. With any luck, those fuckers outside will rip him apart piece by piece. It doesn't look like I'll get a chance with all these other douchebags hanging around.*

Six people had intruded on Dakota's revenge—six people who had no business, no *right*, being there. She had found that shack. She'd dragged Tyler's bound, unconscious body a couple hundred yards over rough terrain. The wheelbarrow she had found inside the shack had gotten them most of the way, but when it tipped over a bump and spilled out Tyler still sixty feet out, she had lacked the strength to lift him by then and had to drag him by his ankles the rest of the way. It had been hard, but she'd proven herself up to the task.

Everything had been going just as she planned it. Dakota had been moments away from avenging her brother.

Then who, of all people, ruined everything? Mark. As if she didn't already have enough reasons to hate him, the fucker had been stalking her.

She couldn't look at him without reliving the night she had woken face down in a pool of her own vomit, Mark on top of her, thrusting away with his little cock. He had finished before she had the chance to fight him off, though a bloody gash in his face showed that she'd tried before she passed out.

He acted like it was the funniest thing when he threw her panties in her face and told her to clean herself up. She had passed back out then, but she remembered.

Humiliation. Revulsion. Despair.

She'd wanted to kill herself after that. Ashamed of her drunkenness and her degradation, she filed no reports and pointed no fingers, instead retreating into herself, wallowing in the emptiness. She couldn't count how many creative ways she had contrived for killing herself. In the end, she chose the most clichéd way of exiting the world and her pathetic life.

But as she lay naked in her bathtub, holding the razor against her wrist, she found that she wasn't completely empty after all. A structure had risen from the shambles of her soul, not quite proper and certainly not whole. It had room only for one thing: anger.

Dakota started to dwell on all those who had done her wrong. She shouldn't have to die while they went on living, perhaps even enjoying the damage they had done. When she thought about Tyler, it made her hit things, lots of things, wishing each one was him.

She made a list—"People Who Should Fucking Die!"—and checked it often. Tyler earned the top spot. She added the "friend" who had abandoned her at the frat party and the people with whom she'd been drinking and drugging. She added her dealer, remembering all the coke he helped into her nose. That was her fault, she knew, but in killing him, she would be doing a public service.

Of course, she couldn't forget Mark. He was a close second to Tyler. Her blood roiled whenever she thought of that son of a bitch. Dakota had never gotten the chance to fight back, not the way she wanted to. If she could have, Mark wouldn't still be alive.

Talk was cheap. She knew that. It was one thing to say she'd kill the bastard and another thing entirely to go through with it, but she had learned a lot about herself that night in the cabin. What she had done to Tyler was proof positive she had the strength to go through with it.

*Tyler.*

Everything was his fault. He was responsible for everything that had happened to Dakota in the last six years. Before a bullet had taken her brother's life, Stevie had always looked out for her. He kept her away from drugs and alcohol and boys like Mark. When Stevie fell, he didn't fall alone. Dakota plummeted into an abyss of her own creation.

*Tyler's creation.*

Tyler's action had torn her world apart, pushed her toward alcohol, into dulling her pain by the bottle, and when the bottle wasn't enough, ecstasy and cocaine filled the void. Half the time, she didn't know what she had taken.

The drugs had led to blackouts. The blackouts led to blacker things. They led to Mark.

Dakota had wanted to die. She couldn't cope with her brother's death or the violence that had taken him from her. After that night with Mark, she only wanted to kill. If she hadn't drunk so much, Mark would never have even… no, it was *his* fault. He was a deviant little fucker who had taken advantage of a defenseless girl.

Well, Dakota wasn't defenseless anymore. She no longer drank or used. She no longer wallowed in depression and self-pity. She no longer filled her void with drugs but with sharp knives and thoughts of revenge.

*Maybe tonight is a blessing in disguise. Kill two fuckwads with one stone… or any other weapon I can get my hands on.*

Dakota shuddered. Every so often, her thoughts frightened her. Was she a killer? Maybe. But if she killed Mark or Tyler, it would be justice, not murder.

And there Tyler stood, still feigning innocence and claiming his crime had been an accident. No one would accidentally shoot a running man from thirty-plus yards away. Dakota could kill him before anyone there could stop her. She doubted they would stand in her way as she went for the door with her bloodied knife in hand. She could walk away, head toward whatever came next, and reinvent herself, leaving Dakota Coogan behind her.

*If those worm things weren't outside.* Those creatures promised only death. For most of the people present, she would welcome that—and worse. But the park ranger had asked for her help. His plea had made it all too real for her that the situation was bigger than her own grudges. She could let the worms take Mark and Tyler, and even herself if necessary, but she couldn't abandon innocents to a horrifying death.

She relaxed her grip on her knife. "Okay," she whispered. "For now."

"Guys," Frosh called. Dakota had never seen him before that night. He looked to be about sixteen and not done growing, though he was probably closer to Dakota's age, nineteen. Mark, the twins, and Tyler were all in their early twenties, the same age as her brother would have been. Abigail was a little older. Merwin could have been her grandfather. His hair was not yet entirely gray, though his mannerisms and body language suggested more virility than his appearance did. He looked like an emaciated hillbilly, but he had presence. When he spoke, people listened, including Dakota.

"I've found something," the kid said.

Tyler's attention diverted away from her. Dakota let her gaze linger a bit longer. She was always suspicious, expecting his demons to emerge. She remembered her brother's wounds. She had insisted upon seeing him at that morgue. Stevie had been grotesquely disfigured, and his wounds had been inflicted *pre*-mortem, *pre*-gunshot wound. The bullet hole had only been the cherry atop a whole shit sundae.

Dakota had wondered then what kind of monster could mutilate a man as if he were meat on a chopping block. Her monster had always had a name: Tyler Kendrick.

Sizing up Tyler now, she couldn't see how he could have disfigured her brother like that. She shook her head, quashing her doubt. The bullet didn't lie. She couldn't question Tyler's guilt, not now, not ever. That psycho had shot her brother, and she had to see that pain returned. It was all that drove her forward.

But first, to deal with those fucking slug things. If they ate Dakota, she wouldn't have her revenge. If they ate Mark and Tyler first, perhaps she'd salute them as foot-long harbingers of righteousness. Somehow, she doubted the creatures were such picky eaters. They'd take everyone, not just the assholes.

So it was up to her to stay alive longer than her enemies. That sounded simple enough. Maybe the kid had found something to help her achieve that goal. Everyone stared down at the kid's feet. Dakota joined them to see what all the fuss was about.

Frosh's foot slid over a small metal clasp. It looked like a handle for a dresser drawer.

"Let's get it open," Bo said, bending over the handle. He wiped the dust away from the cracks, revealing a square approximately two feet wide carved into the floor. "Maybe it's a way out."

"That door there is no way out," Merwin said. "Nothing good can come from a hole in the floor. There ain't no reason for a shack like this to have a cellar. And if that's what it is, cellars are dark, dank places. They're great breeding grounds for nasty things."

"Well, we can't just hang in here until those things decide to come in after us. We're sitting ducks."

"The ogre has a point," Tyler said.

"Thanks… wait—"

Tyler didn't wait for Bo to work it out. "It can't hurt to see what's down there. Maybe there's a bulkhead. It would be nice to know if there's more than one way in and out of this place."

Merwin stroked is beard. "Okay. We check it out. If anything down there moves that ain't human, we hightail out of there quicker than a rabbit running from a pack of wild dogs."

"I thought you said we were safest in here." Dakota didn't like the idea of opening any doors. Things were quiet outside. She preferred to keep it that way. "Maybe we should just hole up here until morning, like you said."

"She's chicken," Bo said, tapping his brother. Luc laughed.

Dakota smirked. *On second thought, let those things on in.*

"She's smart," Abigail said. "No one should be going down there. But if you guys want to kill yourselves, be my guest."

"So who's going to open it?" Merwin asked. The ape twins kept quiet. Tyler pushed his way forward.

"I'll do it."

*Oh, this just keeps getting better and better.*

"You sure?" Merwin asked. "I mean, I don't hear nothing down there, but that don't mean there ain't nothing down there."

Tyler nodded.

"Merwin, don't." Abigail's face had gone white again. "You've seen what they can do."

"It'll be okay... I hope. All right, Tyler. I'll cover you as best I can. Open it now, nice and easy."

Everyone except Tyler took a step back. Dakota held her breath. She held her knife out in front of her, wishing it were a chainsaw. Merwin aimed his rifle at the trap door. Most of the group stood battle ready, armed with the weapons Dakota had meant for Tyler.

Tyler cracked open the trap door. A musty, damp odor rose into the shack. It smelled like bloated corpses washing up on shore after days at sea. Dakota imagined a horde of faceless mutants moaning and clawing beneath them, waiting for those above to join their ranks in hell. Maybe she'd get lucky and they would just pull in Tyler.

The door rose slowly. The air thickened with moisture. It tasted sour. Dakota covered her mouth, not wanting whatever spores infested that air to get into her lungs.

Other than rank air and a pissed-off spider or two, nothing hideous sprang from the opening. Still, Dakota kept her distance. She'd watched enough documentaries to know that some predators let their prey come to them.

Tyler peeked into the opening. "It's pitch-black down there. I can't see a thing."

To Dakota's surprise, Abigail inched closer. She was the last person Dakota expected to see near that hole in the floor. She crouched behind Tyler and pulled her key ring from her pocket. Attached to it was a small penlight. She clicked it on and shined its light into the darkness below.

Tyler nodded his appreciation. "There's water. I can't tell how deep it is. There's a ladder leading down."

He stood. Abigail leaned away from the opening but kept her light shining on it. Tyler walked over to the table where the lantern sat. Before he could grab it, Mark's hand latched onto his wrist.

"That stays up here." Mark released his grip. "Frosh, give him your flashlight."

Frosh hesitated then pulled out the flashlight he had tucked into his back pocket. He handed it to Tyler but was slow to release it when Tyler grabbed it.

"You sure you want to go down there?" Merwin asked.

"I know I don't," Abigail said.

Tyler let out a breath. He looked Dakota straight in the eye. Then he got down on his belly and slid feet first into the hole.

Dakota watched him disappear. *Oh no, you don't.* A hollow feeling came over her. She followed Tyler down the hole, not yet willing to let him out of her sight.

The rungs of the ladder creaked beneath her weight. They were damp and rotting like the rest of the shack—maybe worse—but they didn't break.

At the bottom of the ladder, Dakota plopped down into ankle-deep water. It was icy and filled her sneakers. She shivered. As she walked toward Tyler, the water rose halfway up her shins. Her hand tightened around her knife's grip. Tyler's back was to her. All she had to do was—

"What do you see?" Abigail called from above. She pointed the beam at Dakota, who suddenly felt small.

Tyler threw out a hand, signaling for Dakota to stay back. Her eyes followed the path of his flashlight's beam as it circled four clay walls. It stopped on the wall to her right.

"There's an opening."

Tyler shined his flashlight into an arched passageway that resembled the entrance to a doghouse. Its lowest point was about three feet up the wall. Dakota thought she might be able to crawl through it.

The thought made her uneasy. There was no telling if an animal had claimed that awful spot for its home. *What if those things lived in it?* The idea of having to fend off those creatures in such close quarters made her claustrophobic. Dakota wanted nothing to do with it.

"Let's check it out." Tyler moved toward the opening but didn't get far before tripping. Breaking his fall with his hands, he barely kept his face out of the water.

"Tyler?" Despite how it might have sounded, Dakota was far less concerned about her enemy than whatever had caused him to fall.

"Everything okay down there?" Merwin called.

"We're fine." Tyler stood, his face red with embarrassment. He had managed to hold on to the flashlight, and it was still working. Nothing appeared to be broken, though his clothes were drenched down the front. Dakota stared at him, her brow creasing.

"I'm fine," he said, apparently mistaking her curiosity for worry. "Just wet." He twisted the front of his tattered T-shirt into a knot and watched as the fabric oozed out rancid water.

"What do I care?"

"Don't sound so disappointed. That water can't be good for my insides. It'll probably speed along an infection." Tyler pointed to where Dakota has stabbed him deepest. He smirked. "You may kill me yet."

"I wouldn't bet against it."

Tyler shrugged and laughed, but she heard no humor in it. She could tell all the others were afraid, no matter how each of them tried to hide it. Tyler, though, was unreadable. It was as if everything that had happened to him that day was no different from any other day of his sicko life. She wished she could borrow his indifference.

Tyler squatted. "I tripped over..." He splashed around in the dark water. "This!" He pulled an object from the depths. It was long and narrow and smooth like a cane.

Dakota covered her mouth, immediately recognizing the object for what it was—bone. If she had to guess, she would have pegged it as part of a human leg, a thighbone probably, chipped all over and broken at its end.

Tyler examined it as if it were some curious relic, his face reflecting none of the horror Dakota felt. He had to know what it was, yet he didn't drop it. Instead, he walked with it farther into the cellar, waving it in front of him like a blind man would his cane. In his other hand, he aimed his flashlight's beam low.

"There are more of them," he said matter-of-factly. "A lot more."

Dakota crept up behind him, trying to disturb the water as little as possible. When he stopped suddenly, she bumped into his back. The collision caused the water to slosh, sending miniwaves in all directions. Like a tremor on a spiderweb, the vibrations of the water were sure to be felt by anything living in it.

She turned around. The square opening was like the sun parting the gloom, but it was far away.

*Why the hell did I follow him down here?*

Tyler fixed his flashlight on a mound against the far wall. Dakota peeked around him and stifled a shriek. She shut her eyes and prayed that they had played a trick on her, that they didn't see what her mind told her they'd seen.

But when she opened her eyes, the bones were still there, degrading and void of tissue, piled high in the corner. Dakota recognized the skulls of cats and squirrels. Others came from larger animals. A fair share were undeniably human.

Black specks skittered away from the light. Other things slithered away across the water or sank beneath the surface. Everywhere on the mound, yellow larvae squirmed.

"We shouldn't be down here," Dakota whispered.

"I think you're probably right."

Tyler turned. The flashlight's beam spun with him. It hit upon something Dakota hadn't noticed when she had examined the pile, something mixed in with the bones—a flash of color, nothing more.

"Wait. Let me see that," she said.

Tyler handed her the flashlight. She pointed it at the pile and illuminated something green and mostly obscured. She inched toward the pile. The floor seemed rockier the closer she came to the object, and she knew she had found the pile's beginnings. Bone cracked under her feet, her every step snapping it like peanut brittle.

A moment later, the green object was within her reach. Dakota just had to stick her hand into a heap of dead things to get it. Without letting herself stop to think, she punched her fist into the gap between the bones. When she pulled her hand back out, it held a purse.

A millipede uncoiled and crept out of the partially opened zipper. Its sudden appearance startled Dakota, but she was hardly squeamish. If the human-animal graveyard hadn't turned her stomach, a harmless bug wouldn't do the trick either. She flung the millipede aside and reached into the purse.

Inside it, she found what she had been looking for. Her hand withdrew a thin wallet. Behind a shield of lamination, someone's personal identification was hidden. She wiped the grime from its plastic covering, revealing a Kansas driver's license several years expired.

"Melanie Sullivan," Dakota read aloud. The name brought back memories. So did the face that matched it. They reminded her of all the pain that had led her to Galveston State Park earlier that day, the anguish she wanted Tyler to feel. She struggled to maintain her composure.

"That name mean something to you?"

Dakota spun around. "Don't pretend it doesn't mean anything to you, you sick fuck. Or didn't you care enough to learn the name of my brother's girlfriend before you carved her up?"

She swiped her knife through the air, mimicking what she thought Tyler had done to Melanie. He jumped back, throwing his hands up in defense. Old grief overcame her, and her arms grew heavy. She turned her face away from him. She would never let Tyler see her cry.

"Easy!" Tyler splashed backward, almost tripping over himself. "Your brother's girlfriend?" His forehead folded like an accordion, his eyebrows shooting high and arching. "How should I know her? Look around you. Look at all these bones. You can't really think that I did all of this?"

Dakota wanted to blame him, especially for her brother and his three missing friends. After passing six years convinced of Tyler's guilt, she wanted to cling to her beliefs despite the growing evidence to their contrary, evidence that shook the foundations of her world. Dakota was finding it harder and harder to deny that the cellar looked like some sort of lair, the bones left over from years of feasting. How could she fit Tyler into this puzzle?

Her head started to spin. "I... I don't know." Nausea hit her like a punch to the gut. How could she blame Tyler for all of this when an inexplicable carnivore hunted them outside? Only a monster could have done this. Tyler had shot her brother, but nothing human, not even Tyler, could have done *this*. She looked around at all the bones, wrestling with her thoughts. Her temples pounded.

Finally, the question she dreaded formed in her mind and could not be stopped. *Could I have been wrong all this time?*

Her knees went weak. Dakota leaned over, placing her hands on her thighs for support. Her lunch threatened to expel itself, but after a few dry heaves, she began to collect herself. Tyler crooked his arm beneath hers to help her stand. She pushed him away.

Her stubbornness gave her strength. She thrashed at the pile, knocking bones from it until other objects began to appear. Some jewelry, a jacket, a baseball cap—when she came upon the latter, she shrieked, certain it had been her brother's. Tears welled behind her eyes. Still, she would not let them free.

She picked up the cap and examined it then tucked it into her back pocket. "Let's get out of here," she said, unable to look Tyler in the eye as she handed him back the flashlight.

"Okay, but first, I want to check out that hole. It could be a way out. If you want to head back up, I understand."

Dakota didn't feel right about Tyler being nice to her. If she was wrong, if he hadn't killed her brother... she couldn't think about it. She already had enough wrongs to live with.

"Maybe we should just leave it alone. This place is seriously creeping me out."

Too late. Tyler was already poking his light into the opening. "Wait. I think I see something."

"Nothing alive, I hope."

Tyler's upper torso disappeared into the hole. "It's a little tight for me." His voice became muffled, vibrating into the room like a bass drum after a good whack. "I think it's some kind of tunnel. I can see moonlight shining through the other end. If I were smaller, I might be able to squeeze through there and go get help."

"Get out of there," Dakota whispered.

She didn't like that tunnel. Everything about it seemed wrong. Why weren't the slug things crawling all over it? Maybe they had burrowed the damn thing in the first place. Her dad had told her old war tales about tunnels like that in Vietnam. He had seen the "rats" that went into them, always the smallest guys in the unit. Sometimes, different rats came out. Sometimes, no rats came out at all.

And if there weren't Viet Cong crawling in them, rats of the four-legged kind were there, ravenous vermin placed there by the enemy as biological weapons. Snakes and other nasty critters infested those tunnels, and they weren't the worst of it. As her father had explained it, the tunnel rat went in with a rope tied around his ankle. He crawled on his elbows, with a flashlight and a pistol, deeper into darkness. If an attack came above, the rat was as good as lost, buried alive in a foreign shithole. Alone in suffocating darkness.

Tyler broke in on her thoughts. "Maybe that kid upstairs can crawl in here and see where it goes."

"That's a terrible idea." Dakota had little time to consider it. Dull thudding came from upstairs. She ran to the ladder. "What's going on?"

"Those things are back." Abigail sounded frantic. The noise above grew louder. "They're pounding on the walls. I'm not sure how much longer they'll hold. Any luck down there?"

"We've found a possible way out, but only the kid is small enough to squeeze through it."

"Is it safe?"

Tyler shrugged. "Who knows? Is anywhere? Do we have any other options?"

Abigail disappeared. She returned a moment later and climbed down the ladder. Frosh followed, then Mark. The twins and Merwin stayed above, claiming to keep an eye on the door, but when Dakota looked up, she saw all three of their solemn faces staring down at her. Had they missed their chance to leave by the front door? Merwin's face said as much.

"You," Tyler said, grabbing Frosh by the arm. "What's your name again?"

"It's B—"

"It's Frosh," Mark said, snapping. "You know the rules. You haven't earned your name until I say you have."

Dakota rolled her eyes. "Really? This is hardly the time for your fraternity crap."

"It's okay," the kid smiled. "Frosh is fine."

"Guys? If I could have your attention..." Tyler frowned. The others quieted. "That's better. Frosh, do you think you can crawl through there?" He pointed at the tunnel.

Frosh walked over to the opening. He inspected every wall, ran his fingers along the bottom. "I suppose I could if I had to."

"You have to," Mark said.

"No one is making you do anything," Dakota replied. The look she shot Mark and Tyler was enough to tell them to back off. Mark spat out a sound of derision.

Tyler nodded. "You know what's going on up there better than most of us. You got a look at those things. You know what they can do. I wouldn't wish that fate on any one of you."

He leaned in closer to Frosh. "But it sounds like those things are preoccupied with the walls above. Hell, they'll probably break through any minute now. You may be our best hope for survival. Worst-case scenario, you fail and you're dead. If you don't go, you're dead anyway. We all are."

Frosh nodded. He seemed to be drinking the Kool-Aid, but he made no attempt to get into the opening.

Tyler continued. "You get out there, and you run like the Devil is on your heels. Never look back. Your life, *our* lives, may depend on it." He cracked a smile. "No pressure."

Dakota shook her head. "How will he know how to get back? Even if he escapes this godforsaken place, even if he gets past those godforsaken worms, he may just end up lost in the woods. That won't help anyone."

"I've got a pretty good sense of direction," Frosh said, standing a little taller.

*Men—always trying to play the heroes.* She looked at Frosh, then Tyler, then Mark. *Not a brain among them.*

"It's getting really dicey up here," Merwin yelled. "The

walls are shaking. If you fellas got any bright ideas, now's the time to put them into action."

Unblinking, Frosh stared at the tunnel. Dakota could only imagine the terrible thoughts running through his head and what those small, brave men in her dad's platoon must have thought. *Don't go in there,* Dakota silently willed. Her gut told her that the tunnel was worse than anything going on above.

"Like I said, no pressure." Tyler tapped Frosh on the arm. "No one's going to think any less of you if you stay right here. We'll just have to hunker down and pray those things will pass us by."

"He has to do it," Mark said, pushing his way between Tyler and Frosh. His lips were inches from the boy's ear, but Dakota heard him fine when he said, "If you do this, and you get out, get *us* out, you're an Alpha Pi. Initiation over, just like that."

"Mark, you can take your whole damn fraternity and stick it up your ass for all I care." Frosh stood toe-to-toe with the college senior. "When this is all over, I want nothing to do with you or your stupid group."

Mark looked stunned. He was speechless.

Frosh turned to Dakota. "I'm going, but only because *she* might need help." He nodded toward Abigail, who hung back by the ladder. "She's worth more than all of you put together."

Abigail looked away. "Don't go in there on my account," she said softly.

"I'll be okay. The cabin faces the path leading toward the lake area. That's where Abigail told me Merwin left his Jeep. It's probably not working, but at least it'll be sitting on the path that leads out. I'll circle clear of the building, head toward the Jeep, drive it out if I can, or run like the wind to safety if I can't. I'll get help. I promise."

Dakota had to smile. She admired the little shit. His balls were bigger than the rest of him, and they were rock solid. She had no doubt he meant every word he said.

But words were fragile sounds floating on a fickle breeze. Putting them into action required more than just bravery. With those blood-sucking sons of bitches directly above them, Frosh's plan would require a great deal of luck.

"Mark, give him your flashlight." Tyler's tone made clear he wasn't asking.

Mark snapped out of his stupor. "What? No way, man. Give him yours. It was his to begin with."

"This one is too big. He can hold yours in his mouth while he crawls."

Before Mark could utter another word of protest, Dakota snatched the flashlight out of his hand and gave it to Frosh. "There. That's settled."

"Dakota," Tyler said. "Grab the rope."

She felt her cheeks blush. *You mean the rope I used to string you up earlier so that I could torture you?* "Why?"

"Please, just get it."

She nodded and fled toward the ladder. Halfway up, she asked someone to get her the rope. Luc responded. She wasn't surprised he knew where to find what she needed, since it had been wrapped around his neck. She looped the rope around her arm and carried it to Tyler. Meekly, she handed it over.

He said, "Okay, Frosh. I'm going to tie this around your ankle."

*You can't be serious.* Dread smothered Dakota like a heavy blanket as she thought again of the horrors her father's platoon had endured. Frosh was their tunnel rat.

"You won't be able to crawl backward, so if you see any sign of trouble, lie flat and point your toes toward us. We'll pull you out."

*Just like Dad's stories...*

"The rope is only so long. After a certain point, you'll be on your own."

*Don't go in there.*

Frosh didn't seem keen on the idea, but he let Tyler make the knot. "Wish me luck," he said, flashing a phony smile.

"Don't..." Dakota's objection came too late. Frosh shoved the end of the flashlight in his mouth and crawled into the tunnel. He disappeared, off to face the darkness alone.

She watched as the rope slid through Tyler's hands in steady increments. Foot by foot, it slithered into the opening.

"Do you see anything?" Tyler asked.

"It's lighter up ahead. I think I can get out... ugh, gross." The tunnel amplified the sounds he made inside it. His words echoed into the chamber, and his breathing sounded like that of a woman in labor.

"Everything okay?" Abigail called from above. Her voice trembled. The air, too, seemed to tremble, as if it were electrified or alive. Dakota could tell Abigail liked the boy. Her face was wrought with worry. After all she had been through and had already lost, this woman still worried for another rather than retreating into herself. It made Dakota feel ashamed.

Other than the noise coming from Frosh, the tunnel was silent. Even the pounding above had stopped. It didn't seem right. The silence filled Dakota with trepidation.

"Something's wrong. Get him out."

"I'm okay." Frosh's voice echoed into the cellar. "It's squishier over here. The mud seeps through my fingers. I thought for a second it moved, but it was just my imag—oh, shit!"

His flashlight went dark.

"What?" Dakota sprinted to the tunnel entrance. Her hands instinctively wrapped around the rope. "What is it?"

"I dropped the light in the mud. Oh—*shit*. Something just fell from the ceiling. It might be nothing." A gurgling, slurping noise carried into the basement, followed by an earsplitting shriek, inhuman. Frosh screamed. "Pull me out! Pull me out!"

Tyler didn't hesitate. He yanked the rope hard. Dakota rushed over to help him. The rope stung her hands as she pulled.

"Get back upstairs," she shouted to Mark and Abigail. "Be ready to close the hatch as soon as we're through it."

She knew, even in the throes of panic, that relying on Mark not to lock them all down in that cellar was as good as trusting a snake not to swallow a mouse. Worrying about that came second. She had to haul Frosh out.

In three more pulls, Frosh came spilling out of the tunnel, sliding along its floor as if it were a waterslide. He was still screaming. Dakota tried to catch him, but when she saw what was on him, her hands instinctively recoiled. He plopped down hard into the shallow water, thrashing and kicking. A black mass clung to his shoulder blade. Several more shot from the opening like bullets. They disappeared in the water at her feet.

She sprinted for the ladder. Abigail was gone, and Mark was halfway out. She bounded up the ladder, feeling the rotted wood bending beneath hand and foot as she charged up the rungs three at a time.

When she reached the top, Merwin was waiting, holding the trap door open. *Thank God for him.* She dove into the room, spun on her belly and reached down the hatch to help anyone who had followed.

An arm came out of the dark. She grabbed it and pulled. The sound of wood splintering came from below, and the weight of the body connected to the arm increased. She strained to hold on.

The weight lessened. Tyler had found his footing. His head popped through the opening. Scrambling to her knees then rolling back onto her feet, Dakota heaved Tyler from the abysmal pit. When he was clear, she dove back to the doorway.

Frosh's head emerged.

The mud slugs were all over him, coating him like the gunk on an expelled placenta. He wailed with all the agony of the dying.

Dakota reached for him. She searched for a spot of flesh to grab. An urgency to save him seized her. She would do all she could for the boy, even if it damned her to his fate.

The trap door crashed down. It cracked against Frosh's skull. His neck bent unnaturally, and his screaming stopped. His grip on the ladder released. He fell into the darkness below and was gone.

Dakota had barely been able to pull her arms back in time, the boy's head having been the only thing preventing them from being crushed beneath the weight of the door. Mark's foot had been its driving force. He stood on top of the door, holding it down as it thumped beneath him.

"It was too late for him," he said. More than a few accusatory eyes were upon him. He wasn't wrong. Still, Dakota hated him for it.

The horrid screeching she had heard come from the tunnel now sounded close. Its timbre, high-pitched and eerie, made her brain rattle in her skull. The sound came from somewhere inside the cabin.

*Oh God, they're inside!*

Then she saw the creature. It fell from the back of Tyler's shin. It didn't appear as though it had sunk its teeth into him.

Tyler stepped cautiously away. Everyone else kept their distance. The creature continued to shriek and pulsate, flopping around on the floor like a fish out of water. It rolled up like a pill bug as if trying to shield itself. The creature shrieked louder. Dakota covered her ears. The sound made her ear drums vibrate and her nose feel wet. Was she bleeding?

Still, she kept her eyes fixed on the creature. It flattened out, revealing its true size. A giant black leechlike animal almost a foot in length stretched like an elastic. It then rocketed from its spot on the floor and bounded from wall to wall. Everyone ducked and dove to stay clear of its erratic path, but it didn't seem to be attacking. There was no rhyme or reason to its movements.

Finally, it crashed against the wall beneath the table, where it rolled up into a ball and went silent.

Abigail approached it. "I think I know what's going on with this thing. We Irish suffer from a similar condition… sort of." She flashed her penlight on the creature, and it instantly began to writhe and screech once more.

She turned the light off and it stopped. "Just as I thought."

"It's photosensitive?" Merwin asked.

"Say what, now?" Bo scratched his head.

Abigail nodded. "It's allergic to light."

# CHAPTER 16

"I doubt it's actually *allergic*. I mean, I suppose it could be." Both terrified and amazed, Abigail stared at the creature. The way it moved, solid yet flowing like water, mesmerized her. Every so often, it would raise an end as if it had a nose with which to sample the air. What was it trying to detect? Was it trying to smell her?

Except the creature didn't have a nose. It didn't have eyes, either. It did have a mouth and spines and circular tentacles, pinkish slithering appendages for attaching itself to prey and sucking it dry. As these creatures had done with her husband.

"I bet it just really hates it." She snarled as she clicked on the flashlight, wanting to make the beast squirm. The creature hissed and retreated flat against the wall, trying to escape the light. If Abigail could have harnessed the power of the sun, she'd have fried the little fucker and its friends outside. She would have burned down the whole damn forest to kill them all.

"You know what they say about dogs backed into corners," Dakota said, gently covering Abigail's hands with hers. "Maybe we should let this sleeping dog lie."

Canine clichés aside, Abigail got the point. She hated that foul slug thing with more hate than she ever thought she could muster. She wanted to kill it, to grind it beneath her heel and listen as its life left it in an agony equivalent to what she had experienced, but she only had one sneaker left, and she doubted it would help her mash the little shit into a flattened mass of black Jell-O.

"Does anyone else feel like that thing is watching us?" Luc stepped next to the girls. Revulsion marked his face.

*It is watching us.* Though she didn't know how, Abigail

knew it was true. "I want to kill it."

Luc nodded. "We definitely should do something. I don't like that thing in here with us."

"We should keep our distance," Merwin said, again the voice of caution.

"Oh, the hell with that." Abigail was fed up with caution. She didn't like the idea of sitting there and waiting for the next wave of worms to batter the walls or swarm up from the basement. Eventually, they would tear down that shack. Then what? Were she and the others going to fend off hundreds of creatures with a handful of flashlights and a single lantern?

No, they had to learn how to fight these things. They had to learn how to kill them. A fire burned inside her. She wanted to see this particular squishy black fucker suffer and die. If she didn't kill it soon, she knew the fire within would consume her.

Dakota's hands tightened around hers. She shook her hands free, but Dakota reached under her arm and pulled her closer. Abigail strained to twist out of her grasp. "Let me go. Let me kill it. You don't understand." How could this stranger understand what had happened? Abigail had lost a husband, a man she had loved. A man who had fought to save her. A man she had failed.

She buried her head in the crook of Dakota's neck. Finally, the tears came. Abigail found a moment's solace in the stranger's arms.

Merwin raised his gun. His intent was obvious: he planned to send that globular demon straight back to whatever hell it had crawled up from.

"Wait," Bo said. "The noise might bring its friends back. I have a better idea. Luc, remember when those possums would try to nest under our porch?"

Luc scratched at his neck. "Ah, I gotcha."

All eyes were on Bo as he picked up Dakota's duffle bag. He unzipped it and dumped its contents all over the floor.

"Hey, jerk," Dakota protested, but it was already too late. Clothes, water, keys, cigarettes, and her personal belongings littered the floor.

Bo swirled an arm inside the bag. His hand came out, grasping nothing but air. "Good. It's empty. Now I'll just place the open bag beside the table like this." He tiptoed toward the edge of the table. The lantern shone on top of it. Below it, the creature hissed in the only dark place in the room. Bo dropped the bag and shuffled backward. The creature did not move.

"Now, we'll use our flashlights to lure it into the bag."

"That's it?" Mark punched Bo in his arm. "That's your brilliant plan?"

Merwin tugged his beard. "It could work."

"Yeah, Sherlock? And who's going to close the bag once that thing hops inside of it?"

*A fair question.* Abigail's mouth curled into a smile. It seemed to unsettle some of the others. She didn't care. "I will."

She trotted over to the back of the room, where Dakota's crude instruments had been strewn about. Most had vanished. Abigail had no idea who was hiding what instrument but suspected they all were hiding something. It made no difference to her. She wanted the meat hook—an ugly, twisted piece of wrought iron weaponry, like something from a more savage time—which lay right where she had last spotted it. She picked it up and carried it over to the table under which the creature hid.

She crouched down a foot away from the duffle bag, keeping it between her and the vicious bloodsucker, wanting to show it just how vicious the human race could be. "Flush it out."

"It's your funeral." Mark walked away.

Bo crept to the other side of the table and shined his flashlight directly at the creature.

Man, was it pissed! Abigail was quick to regret her decision, but she kept her position. The slug thing gurgled and shrieked, spitting out a clumpy black ooze. Its head rose and swayed back and forth like an enchanted cobra. It seemed intoxicated, or perhaps it was preparing to strike. Abigail couldn't predict its next move. Her doubts grew.

The creature collapsed into itself, pancaking onto the floor. With a speed so quick that Abigail only saw a blur, the creature propelled itself toward the bag.

Toward Abigail.

"Poop," she muttered as the monster flew off the floor. Her

reflexes acted on their own volition. Her arm was swinging before her thoughts could even process why. The pointed metal at its end caught and impaled the creature, now little more than a disgusting worm on an oversized hook.

She dropped both worm and hook into the duffle bag and zipped it shut. That was when Abigail lost her cool. She grabbed the bag's handle and slammed the bag repeatedly into the floor, grunting and howling like an animal. Curse words she wasn't aware she knew sprang from her mouth. For the first time that night, she felt like she was in control. It felt good.

When she'd let out her steam, she glanced at the others, who were staring, openmouthed. She dropped the bag on the floor. The creature inside made only subtle movements, just enough to let her know it was still alive.

"Kill it," she said.

The others swarmed the bag like carrion birds over a fresh kill. Dakota, Mark, and the twins, working together against a common enemy, stabbed and prodded the bag with sadistic zeal. Sharp, pointy weapons rose and fell like the hammers on a piano. They reminded Abigail of the old Eagles song—only this group, stabbing with their steely knives, would certainly kill the beast. She rushed to join them, her bloodlust not yet satisfied.

Only Merwin and Tyler held back. *Fuck them.* She needed this speck of revenge. It might be all she'd get. As she and the others stabbed away, she was amazed that no one took the chance to slice someone else. Some blades hit their mark. The weapons rose covered in oily plasma. Black slime dripped from one twin's screwdriver. Others just hit fabric. The creature shrieked and slashed blindly with its spines. Its struggling slowed.

*Dying.*

Eventually, the bag stopped moving. The arms stabbing at it stopped, too.

A thousand shrieks rose in unison from all around the cabin. Abigail's hands went to her ears. She curled into a ball, the pain in her head debilitating.

The worms went silent. Abigail rose to her feet. "You like

that?" she shouted. "That's for Karl, you bastards!"

Tyler nudged the bag with his foot. It sloshed as if filled with water. He upended it. Sludge pissed out through the zipper. It ran in a narrow, winding river toward the trap door despite there being no noticeable decline in the floor. The liquid disappeared into the cellar. Not a drop remained above. It was as if the creature had never existed.

Tyler opened the bag. Abigail held her breath as he lowered his head to peek inside. She imagined the slug thing popping out of the bag like some twisted jack-in-the-box and tearing Tyler's face into ribbons.

But nothing sprang from the bag. Tyler's face remained one hundred percent intact.

Like a magician displaying an empty top hat, he showed everyone the inside of the bag. It was empty save for an inner lining smeared with mud.

Abigail allowed herself to breathe again. "Where did it go?"

Tyler pointed to the cellar doorway. "It liquefied, I guess."

"You mean it got away?"

Tyler laughed. "No, I'm pretty sure you guys killed it several times over."

Merwin cleared his throat. "Well, I reckon it's settled, then. Those suckers hate light, so it's probably safe to say they're nocturnal. We hunker down here until morning then mosey on out of here when the sun's shining brightly above us."

For once, everyone seemed to be in agreement. Abigail caught Merwin's gaze. He looked at her with a fatherly concern that softened his gaunt features. She faked a smile for his benefit. He looked away, his cheeks a shade rosier.

"Well," he continued, clearing his throat again. He glanced at his watch. "That gives us five or six hours—"

*Abigail.*

"—anyone wants to sleep—"

"Huh?"

*I'm outside, Abigail. It's safe to come out now, baby.*

"—think anyone here will be able to sleep, but—"

"Karl?"

"Is she okay?" Merwin asked.

Abigail closed her eyes. As if the night weren't already fucked, now she was hearing voices. Well, not voices. Just one voice, her late husband's. She opened her eyes and listened. The voice was gone.

Other voices, real voices, were muttering things about her sanity.

"I'm fine," she said firmly. She ran her fingers through her hair. "I guess I'm still a little out of it."

"Abigail!"

She closed her eyes again, willing the voice away. *You're dead. There's not a damn thing I can do about it now. Please, don't haunt me. Let me get out of this mess, and I promise I will grieve for you like a good wife should.*

When she opened her eyes, she noticed that the others had lost interest in her waning sanity. They all stared at the door.

"Abigail! Help me!"

"Who is that?" Dakota asked. "Shouldn't we let him in?"

"Wait? You guys hear him, too?" Abigail tried to process it. She knew that voice as well as she knew her own. But she'd seen him die, hadn't she? Her mind was not yet willing to cling to false hope—but that thing had drugged her. How could she be sure anything she had seen was real? There was no denying that voice.

"Karl?" She took one hesitant step toward the door. "You're alive?"

Her shuffling feet began to walk then quickly escalated into a mad dash toward the door. Karl was *alive*. In a moment, she would open the door and be with him again, hold him in her arms, kiss his soft lips, his lovable fat head.

Strong arms clamped around her, but they didn't belong to her husband. "Wait," said one of the twins. His arms were like a crane, lifting her off the floor. "We don't know what's outside."

"We can't just leave him out there." Dakota, her heroine, rushed to the door. "He needs our help."

"Like hell we can't." Mark blocked her path, his weapon drawn.

"Again with the knife?" Dakota said. "That's getting kinda old already, don't you think?"

"Get out of the way, Mark." Tyler, another hero, stood beside Dakota. If they made it out of that god-awful park alive, Abigail figured she'd owe them big-time. Maybe she'd have them over, fix them a nice dinner. That would be nice—to be back doing normal things. Why couldn't she just be back doing normal things?

*With Karl.*

If they helped her save Karl, Abigail would name her unborn children after Tyler and Dakota. Hell, she'd even name her kid after Merwin. Or her next dog.

Bo, or Luc, had her locked up good. She didn't bother to squirm, figuring he'd be more apt to let her go if she were calm. Her legs already ached from a long day of hiking and running for her life. Conserving her energy seemed like a smart plan. The others would do her dirty work, take the risks.

*Like that boy, that poor, poor boy.*

Abigail found it hard to swallow. "Put me down," she whispered. To her surprise, the twin let her go. When she turned, Abigail saw it was Luc who had grabbed her. She could tell by the unbroken nose.

Luc held her by the wrist, gently. "I'm not saying we shouldn't help him. We just need to be careful about it."

"Well, we know which one of you got the brains." Merwin stepped into the fray, rifle in hand. He cast a sideways glance at Mark. "Put that away, son. The young lady's right—it is getting old."

"What's the plan?" Tyler asked.

"On three, you open the door, and I'll shoot anything that ain't human fixing to get in here." He raised his rifle. "The rest of you might want to stand back a bit."

They all did, except Abigail. She had to see what was out there. Not that it mattered. She'd help Karl no matter what she had to face, with one shoe, no shoes, or no feet at all. She would do her own goddamn dirty work.

*God, don't let my courage fail me now.*

She stood just behind Merwin's right shoulder, close enough to smell Old Spice and man musk. Her fingers dug into his arm, but she couldn't let go. She stared at the door. Tyler reached for the knob.

"One... oh hell. Just open it."

Before anyone could utter another word, Tyler's wrist turned. He swung the door open and hid behind it. Abigail stared out into the night.

The forest was silent. Even the insects seemed to have taken the night off from their chirping and breeding. If Karl was out there, she couldn't see him. Then someone, or something, moved behind a bush. It appeared to be a man, and it might have been Karl, but Abigail couldn't tell. All she could see was a shape rising in the darkness.

"Karl?" Abigail came around Merwin. She inched closer to the threshold.

"Stay back, Abigail. You're blocking my shot."

"Please," a voice said, emanating like a whisper on the wind from the direction of the shadowy figure. It was low, gritty, and echoed in the most unnatural way as if it wasn't one voice but many. "Help."

The figure no longer sounded like Karl, but it sure started to look like him. Even in the darkness, Abigail knew her husband's shape. Thirteen years she had spent sleeping next to that body. Thirteen years, putting up with his mouth-breathing, bed-hogging, blanket-stealing ass. She would have given anything to be back in that bed with her husband.

*Please help me, Abigail. It hurts so bad.*

"Karl? Come inside, Karl. It's safer in here."

"Can't... move... hurt."

"I'm coming, baby." Abigail's legs trembled as she took a step. She crossed the threshold.

"Don't go out there," Merwin said, tugging on the back of the sweatshirt Frosh had given her. "I don't know who or what that is, but I know it ain't your husband."

"I think I would know my own husband." An unsteady laugh escaped her. Her anxiety was undermining her resolve. She couldn't let it. *He needs me.*

"I'm coming, Karl," she muttered again, more to reassure herself than her husband that she'd be stepping out of the light to save him.

"Come back inside." Merwin sounded like he was begging.

"It's fine. I'm fine. He needs me."

Her sneaker squished into mud as she crept toward her beckoning husband. The earth accepted her other, sneakerless foot into its wet confines. The mud coated her sock. Cold water seeped in through the fabric. A few yards ahead, where the light of the doorway faded, the mud seemed deeper, slushier. Its surface looked as if it were boiling.

Karl's voice played like a record in her mind, calling her closer. It battled against another voice, a smaller one. That second voice was telling her what her brain refused to process, the fact her two eyes had witnessed. Her husband was dead.

A third voice, even smaller, whispered from the shadows—there a moment, gone the next, a low hum that, like Karl, beckoned her forward but halted her feet. *Join us*, she thought she heard. *Come join us.*

The figure in every way resembled Karl, or at least a cardboard cutout of him. He said he was hurt, but he was standing. Why wouldn't he move? What had those things done to him?

As she approached, stepping deeper into the oozing earth, Abigail studied the figure. Her husband never moved an inch, not so much as a twitch. It was as if he were a statue, ebony and featureless. Now only twelve feet away, Abigail expected to see the whites of his eyes, the shine of his teeth, the color of his clothes—anything that would mark him human, alive. He remained a black mold, all covered in night, as if he had risen from the mud beneath her feet.

The Karl thing raised a hand.

"I'm here, baby," she said softly. "I'm here."

The hand extended toward her, reaching, growing. Fingers as long as snakes stretched toward Abigail. They were not her husband's. The ground before her boiled more fiercely, and she saw that it was alive. *Slithering.*

"Get back!" someone shouted. The loud blast that followed drove Abigail to her knees, her palms slamming over her ears, but she kept watching. Karl's upper body rocked backward though his feet, hidden behind the bush, remained firmly rooted, as if they were cemented in place. When he righted, he fell to pieces.

No, he exploded into a hundred shrieking leeches.

Abigail turned and ran.

Her eyes grew wide as she stared down the barrel of Merwin's rifle. He squinted through the scope, correcting his aim with slight movements. Still, she raced toward him. Death by firing squad had a much better ring to it than being eaten alive.

The gun trembled in Merwin's hand. Was he afraid to take the shot? The shrieking behind her grew louder. Abigail tucked her head and dove forward onto her hands and knees, back into the light but short of the relative safety of the shack's four walls.

"Shoot!" she yelled.

"At which one?" Merwin asked.

"All of them!"

When the blast came, Abigail closed her eyes and prepared for oblivion, her mind vaguely cognizant of the fact that if the bullet was going to hit her, it would have done so already.

But the bullet had hit something. It sounded like a bee had suicide bombed into a brick wall, ending its life in a satisfying splat.

"What the heck, man?" someone shouted behind Abigail. An arm hooked beneath hers, and she screamed. That thing that had impersonated Karl had her now, but it wouldn't have her without a fight.

"Easy. I'm trying to help you," a man said as he took her elbow into his stomach. She stopped resisting then, and together with a stranger, she stumbled back into the cabin.

Tyler slammed the door shut.

# CHAPTER 17

"He shot me!"

"Charlie?" Tyler couldn't believe who he was seeing. "What are you doing here? You shouldn't be here."

He paced the length of the cabin, running his fingers down his face, chewing his nails down to the pink. When he reached one end of the cabin, he paced back to the other end.

"You know this guy?" Merwin asked.

Tyler stopped pacing just long enough to nod and offer a meek, "He's my parole officer," before resuming his march.

"Wait," Abigail said. "Parole officer? You're a convict?" When Tyler didn't answer, she pushed him. "Do you have something to do with those things outside?"

Merwin held her back. "You're not thinking straight, Abigail. You know he couldn't possibly."

Tyler might have defended himself against the accusation, but his mind was elsewhere. *You should not have come here. Goddamn it, Charlie. Why couldn't you just forget about me?*

He knew why Charlie had come to the park. What other reason could his parole officer have than to bring home his delinquent parolee? Why did he have to tell Charlie where he was going? Did he owe him that much?

*I do owe him that, and then some.*

Charlie had been his only friend since leaving Wichita State Penitentiary. Whatever happened to him that night would be forever on Tyler. He clenched his fists, his chewed, jagged nails digging into his palms. "Shit, shit, shit, *shit!*"

"There's no need for cussing." Charlie's left hand held his right arm tightly. Blood squeezed through his fingers. "I've been shot, and you don't hear me using that language."

Mark rolled his eyes. "Who let in the fruitcake? And what's up with his face?"

"I'll turn the other cheek to that. After the night I've been having..." Charlie wiped the back of his hand across his forehead and frowned then poked absentmindedly at raw wounds on his face. "Whew! There are some ungodly things in these woods. I was attacked by this nasty little critter—some sort of spongy worm. Then, I make my way here, and this guy takes a shot at me." He threw out a finger toward Merwin.

"Yeah, uh, sorry 'bout that."

"Well, lucky for me, you're a lousy shot. Why were you shooting at me anyway?"

"Tonight has been rough going for us, too." Merwin reached toward Charlie, who slapped his hand away. "Let me have a look at that."

Charlie looked at Tyler, who offered him a nod to assure him Merwin was okay. Slowly, the parole officer removed his hand from his sleeve. A patch of blood had formed around a tear in the shirt.

"Hey," Charlie whined as Merwin unstuck the sleeve from the wound. The bullet had carved a shallow, dime-sized basin in Charlie's triceps.

"It looks worse than it is. You'll live." Merwin stroked his beard, not seeming to care that he was smearing Charlie's blood into it. "Well, it won't be the gunshot that will kill you tonight, anyway. What happened to your face?"

Tyler hadn't really looked at Charlie's face since the man barreled into the cabin. Shame and guilt and the horror of knowing Charlie's death could be his fault had kept him from meeting the eyes of his parole officer. He had seen enough to recognize the new arrival as Charlie and to know that he was wounded. Now he raised his head to take in the rest.

What he saw was gruesome. Two strips of black circles ran down Charlie's forehead and cheeks like an allergy test gone horribly wrong. At the midpoint of each circle, the skin was gone, a dark red bull's-eye in its place. From there, hot-pink flesh blended into the peach of living epidermal tissue like the inside of a medium rare steak. Black lines, like veins of ore, extended through the pink muscle. At the edges of each wound, dead skin flaked off like ash.

*What have I done to you?* Tyler gaped at his friend. He bit into his lower lip, fighting back tears.

Charlie must have sensed the eyes upon him. "My face?" he asked as if he could somehow have forgotten that he had been savagely mutilated even as his fingers continued to massage around his injuries. He touched an open sore on his cheek and cringed.

"Yes, I remember. It looks that bad, huh? One of those... those spawns of hell latched onto my face. There was this deer, and..." Charlie shook his head. Tyler couldn't tell if he was trying to piece together the details or was merely having a difficult time sharing them.

Tyler's father's voice intruded. *He'll go through a lot more pain before this night is over.*

"Anyway, that thing attacked me. I fought it off, but it must have released some kind of toxin into me. I blacked out. I can't remember much of the last few hours. Bad dreams mostly. But when my mind cleared, I found myself stumbling toward this cabin, toward the light of your open door."

"That was fortunate," Dakota said. "You're lucky to be alive."

"Lucky?" Charlie made the sign of the cross. "The Big Man must have been looking after me in my hour of need."

"Humph," Merwin uttered. "Well, one thing's for damn sure: we're going to need all the help we can get from the 'Big Man' to make it past those animals."

"What's going on here?" Charlie's voice had softened. Tyler could hear his fear. "What are those things?"

"They're not animals."

"What's that, now?" Merwin stretched his neck to see over the crowd, searching for whomever had spoken those words. Tyler knew who said it. Only two females had the misfortune of being part of their company, and Tyler had yet to hear Dakota's voice be anything but gruff and seething with spite.

He looked for Abigail, and the crowd parted around her. She shrank beneath cold stares. Everyone was silent, waiting to hear what she had to say. She stood, hands folded, her chin buried into her chest, her shoulders bunching up near her ears.

"It was Karl, but *not* Karl. It spoke to me, and not just out there." Abigail pointed to her head. "In here."

"Great." Mark sneered. "The dumb bitch is losing it again."

"Leave her alone, Mark," Luc said, coming to Abigail's rescue. Mark gaped at him, at a loss for words. Even Bo was speechless.

Abigail raised her chin and glared at Mark. "Think what you want. You may not have heard all that I heard, but you heard it talk."

"I didn't hear anything," Mark said. "I wasn't stupid enough to go near it."

"It *did* talk," Dakota said.

"I heard it, too," Tyler added. "At least I think I did."

*Yeah, you heard it talk, buddy,* his father said.

"Now, slow down, everyone." Merwin raised his arms as if he were a mime trapped in an invisible box. "I heard it make sounds, sure. There's no disputing that. And maybe they were words, but that don't mean those things are intelligent life. Hell, I've got a pair of lovebirds that can recite the alphabet, and they crap in their food dish every single day."

Abigail's face reddened. "You can't be serious. It wasn't just mimicking us like some damn parrot. It called to me, and it looked like…"

Her words failed. Dakota rubbed soothing circles into her back.

Merwin tugged on his beard. "I reckon I can't rightly be certain of what I saw and heard. Noise, like words, coming from a dark mound shaped like a man."

"Not just any man," Abigail cried. "You may not have known him long, but come on! And it spoke with *his* voice."

"Okay, okay. Let's assume you're right. If those dirty devils are so smart, what's keeping them from figuring out a way in here and having themselves a Thanksgiving feast?"

"It's the light," Dakota said. "We know that already."

"So you're telling me that those things can think like us, even impersonate us, yet the only reason we ain't deader than roadkill is because of one stupid lantern light? I'm sorry, but I just don't believe—"

"Ugh!" Charlie crumpled over himself, his arms tucked in against his sides like a running back protecting the ball. He had a look on his face, as if he couldn't decide if he wanted to vomit or shit his pants right then and there. His eyes bulged, and his face turned a deep purple as he strained to hold it in.

He heaved and covered his mouth. Nothing came out.

"You okay?" Merwin asked.

When Charlie heaved again, that *Oh shit*, wide-eyed-but-empty stare blanketed his eyes. Again, he covered his mouth with the back of his hand. This time, when he coughed, he spattered his hand with blood.

"Oh God! Oh God, no!"

Tyler went to help his friend, but Merwin held him back. The rest of the crowd watched from beyond Charlie's reach. One look at Charlie was all anyone needed to know he wasn't right.

His body jerked. Drool ran from his mouth as his stomach grumbled. Shaking fingers fumbled to undo his shirt's top button. It came undone, exposing a white T-shirt beneath. He worked his way down the buttons in between spasms, muttering prayers, begging for God's help. His eyes found Tyler. They pleaded for an end to what ailed him.

*God won't help him now.* Tyler's father laughed inside his head. *You did this to him, Tyler. You led him here.*

Charlie had all but the last button undone when his head jerked sideways. He arched backward at a severe angle only a contortionist could maneuver safely, a whimper passing his lips as his body snapped, crackled, and popped like Rice Krispies. His stomach protruded toward the ceiling. He rocked back onto his heels.

Tyler broke the line and rushed to Charlie's aid. He placed a hand on his parole officer's back to prop him up. Something beneath Charlie's skin moved. It felt like an organ had come loose and was rummaging around in Charlie's body.

Tyler let go of his friend and slowly backed away. *I'm sorry, Charlie.* His father's voice inside him laughed on.

Charlie shot upright. His face contorted in terror, and his tongue rolled back into his mouth. He gasped. "I can't feel my legs!"

Yet there he stood, there he walked, like some trapped puppet dangling from the fishhooks of an angry god. Everyone kept their distance, giving him freedom to roam.

"Stop me!" Charlie yelled. "They're controlling me. Oh God, oh God, oh God. The Devil is inside me!"

By the time Tyler fully understood the meaning behind his friend's words, it was too late. Charlie had already reached the lantern. As he raised it over his head, his open shirt revealed a pregnant stomach. His babies skittered beneath the skin.

Charlie screamed. A dark black mass cut its way out of his stomach. Charlie smashed the lantern against the floor and stomped on it. The light went out.

# CHAPTER 18

Running.

Abigail wondered if there would ever be an end to it. Well, surely, if those things caught her…

*Better not to think of it. Better to just run.*

Bo had been the first out the door when the light went out. The creatures had been waiting. They'd swarmed him, covering his skin, like ants on a piece of candy that had fallen in the dirt. Any brains they might possess were trumped by insatiable hunger. They'd ripped through Bo like sharks through chum.

His hollering for help, his anguished pleas for his brother, anyone, filled the night air with a soundtrack Abigail couldn't block out. She didn't help him. No one did, not even his twin brother.

Instead, they ran. Bo had taken one for the team. His screams had accentuated Abigail's shame.

*Better not to think of it. Better to just run.*

Her penlight was all the protection she had against an army of those mud-skipping motherfuckers. She saw them everywhere, even the places they weren't, and heard them nipping at her heels. The flashlight's beam half circled up in front of her then moved behind her with the sway of her arm. She tried to aim the beam erratically with each backswing to keep those leech bastards guessing. Because if even one got past that pathetic excuse for a light—

*Better not to think of it. Better to just run.*

Cool air rushed into her lungs. Hot air came out. Abigail wondered how long her legs would hold up after all they had been through, or her feet after all the punishment they'd endured. She had let the mud take her remaining sneaker as soon as she exited the shack, knowing she'd be faster barefoot. Her endurance surprised her, but she knew it couldn't last.

*Maybe I don't need to hold up the longest. Maybe I just can't be the slowest.*

The thought of the others vying with her, and she with them, in a game of survival of the fittest made the horror worse. She wished Karl were still with her. No, she didn't want Karl to have to suffer all over again. She didn't wish her predicament on anyone else any more than she wished Karl's and Bo's and Frosh's fate on herself.

*Better not to think of it. Better to just run.*

"The trail is this way!" Merwin shouted between gasps. He was up ahead, but Abigail was gaining on him. Another man was running to her right. She didn't sneak a glance to see who it was for fear it might slow her down.

Pain shot through Abigail's soles with every footfall. Twigs and rocks and only God knew what else stabbed at her feet and shredded her socks. She took each stride, wondering what would trip her next or puncture her flesh. The pain spurred her forward, kept her alert and alive.

*Better not to think of it. Better to just run.*

She lengthened her stride.

Abigail passed Merwin and kept on running. The ranger almost seemed happy for it. "Go!" he shouted. "Follow the trail, and never stop running. Never look back!"

Abigail's thoughts exactly. With every second, she increased the distance between herself and the ranger, but that wasn't the distance that concerned her. She hurdled some roots and exploded out of the forest and into the moonlight. Finding the path was a small achievement, but Abigail clung to it. Small insects—gnats or fruit flies or something like them—clouded around her head and caught in her saliva as she sucked in air. Her body itched all over. She had probably fattened dozens of mosquitos, but being eaten by those blood-sucking pests was a far cry better than even one bite from—

*Better not to think of it. Better to just run.*

Frogs croaked to her right, telling her the lake was not far off. Abigail wasn't heading that way. She turned left and pumped harder down the trail. The ground was uneven, filled with treacherous hills and hard-to-see valleys, but at least the surface was soft, the thick grass cushioning her feet.

Grunting and heavy breathing followed behind her. Abigail didn't know who made the sounds, but she knew they were human, and that alone was comforting. If people were behind her, she had succeeded in creating a buffer zone between her and that which hunted her.

Unless those mud fucks knew a shortcut.

*Better not to think of it. Better to just run.*

Abigail passed a car parked in the middle of a trail. Its doors were open, and something dead lay in front of it. She didn't even slow down to see if it was her ticket out of that awful place. Those monsters had destroyed Merwin's Jeep. She wasn't willing to risk precious time on the slim chance that the abandoned Chevy hadn't been dealt a similar fate.

On and on she ran. It wasn't long before she reached the campgrounds. Summoning her breath, she screamed for help but continued running down the trail. The lots were too risky. They probably had just one way in and one way out with no guarantee of refuge.

But campgrounds meant people, and people meant civilization—a place where no footlong, flesh-eating leeches latched themselves to a girl's back or ate her husband. Abigail's eyes began to tear up, but she blinked them dry. The thought that she might actually survive the night crossed her mind.

*Definitely better not to think of it,* she cautioned herself as if thinking would jinx her luck. *Better to just run.*

"Head to the camper," a voice wheezed behind her. "We can hole up there."

*Camper? It would have more light than this pathetic thing.* She glanced at her flashlight and frowned. What she needed was a lightsaber, but Abigail held firmly to what light she had. She had no doubt that even that three-inch, one-battery, plastic piece of shit had saved her life a few times as she ran.

She slowed and chanced a peek over her shoulder. Two figures ran side by side behind her, one tall and burly, the other short and wiry.

*Mark and Luc.* Of all people to have at her side when death was chasing her, why did it have to be those assholes?

She cursed her endless stream of misfortune. Abigail knew she couldn't trust them, especially not the small, shifty little bastard. Maybe she was better off keeping to her running. It had kept her alive so far.

Then she found her silver lining. Though no one followed behind the two boys—and by that point, she had to assume the others were dead—she saw none of those slimy noodles, either.

*Better not to think of it.* It was too late. The jinx was in. *Here they come.*

On any other night, Abigail might have blamed the wind for the rustling in the brush, but not that night—a night with few breezes but many slimy noodles. Marc and Luc darted into one of the camping areas. Acting more on instinct than thought, Abigail followed them, hoping the college delinquents had some semblance of an idea, some half-cocked notion that just might keep her alive. Those mud fucks were close now. Her time to make her final stand would soon come.

*Chances for survival? None to none.* Abigail laughed uneasily. *Slim* had gone by the wayside.

"Shit! Somebody popped the tires!"

*Not somebody, Luc.* Abigail huffed. *Guess we're not driving out of here.* From the trail, she couldn't make out the boys or their camper. A few more yards, and she'd be at the clearing. Behind her, from the direction of the shack, a tidal wave of leeches surged toward her, juggernauting its way through the trees.

"Who cares right now?" Mark said. "Would you rather stay out here? Get inside, and turn on every fucking light."

Abigail ran into the lot just in time to see Mark closing the camper door. He paused, his eyes making contact with hers for only a moment, enough time for her to see the measure of a man—and recognize her late husband's worth. Karl wouldn't have closed the door until she was safely inside. Mark barely hesitated before slamming it shut.

*You worm.* Mark had seen her. Abigail was sure of it, and

she had nowhere left to go. She ran to the motor home and tried the door. It was locked.

"Let me in, you asshole!" she shouted, pounding on the door. The rustling grew louder. The creatures drew nearer, their screeching carrying before them, toward the warmth of human blood.

They poured in from everywhere.

"Open the door!" Abigail cried. The sound of an engine, then a loud crash, came from somewhere nearby on the trail. She pounded harder on the camper door.

"Sorry, this one's occupied. Better try the next one."

The unearthly voices of the pursuing monsters pulsed through her like the blood in her veins. Sweat and tears fought to see which could blind her first. A gunshot rang loud and clear and close. Her heart beat at her chest as if it wanted what she wanted—to escape.

*Not into the camper. Not toward what's behind it. Not back down the trail.*

Into the woods again. That was her only option, thanks to Mark. Abigail wasn't the violent type, but she swore that if they both somehow made it through the night, she would hunt down Mark and kill him. But that was something she could think about later. There was no time for it now.

The leeches were coming.

*Better to just run.*

# CHAPTER 19

Dakota spit dirt from her mouth. Her tongue tingled with pain. She could feel the imprints of her teeth in it after her chin's collision with the ground. The ache dulled her other senses. She shook her head on straight. She hadn't seen who had tripped her, but she could make a fairly educated guess.

Scrambling to her feet, full of rage and spitfire, Dakota was ready to hunt down that bastard Mark. He wouldn't be leaving those woods alive. Her hostility eased a bit when she felt hands helping her up.

"Tyler?" Dakota couldn't believe it—she was happy to see him. After all she had done to him, Tyler wouldn't leave her behind. "Thanks," she said softly. The dark hid her blushing cheeks, but she couldn't hide the tone of humility in the one word she'd offered him. It sounded more like an apology than an expression of gratitude.

"Don't mention it," Tyler said, dragging her forward. His fingers were harsh around her arm, ripping her from the ground. "No time for talk. Move!"

If time had slowed after her fall, it now shot into overdrive like that moment in every war film after a grenade explodes and the slow-motion sequence ends. The sounds of human suffering bellowed in her ears. Reality, in all its harshness, had returned like a knife to her stomach.

*Tyler would know a little something about that.* He should have left her in his dust. Yet there he ran, glued to her side, urging her forward.

The others were gone, all except Bo, whose wails at last gave way to the Pale Rider, come to collect another soul for the underworld. Bo was fortunate that it was over, anyway. No more malevolent terrors awaited him in the woods. Maybe it was worse where he had gone, but somehow, Dakota doubted it.

"Do you know where we're going?"

"Not a clue." Tyler coughed. He panted his words out between breaths. "But... you don't want to... go back... that way." He threw a thumb over his shoulder.

"The trail is this way!" Merwin shouted somewhere in front of them. She strained to see anything beyond ten or twelve feet. The night was thick beneath wide branches fat with leaves. *Come on, Merwin. Where are you?*

Tyler shifted left. Dakota followed, hoping he could see what she couldn't. She had enough trouble trying to see the roots reaching out to trip her.

"Go!" Merwin's voice blasted through the air. "Follow the trail, and never stop running. Never look back!"

"There." Dakota pointed. "It's Merwin!"

Again, they adjusted their course—and nearly ran straight into a wave of hissing and slithering monsters. One crossed in front of Dakota. The filthy shit reared its ugly head back, exposing its suckers. The tentacles writhed like snakes.

With her front foot rolling onto its toes, Dakota launched herself into the air. The globular leech folded in upon itself. Dakota thought it was ducking to avoid a collision. She *thought* she'd hurdle it easily.

Not so. The creature went from shit pancake to shit bamboo shoot, stretching high with uncanny timing. Like an elastic that had been released, the creature's elongated frame collapsed inward, resulting in a globe that rocketed straight up. It hovered in the air just long enough for Dakota's unstoppable momentum to carry her into it.

She saw its spine protract like cat claws. With no weapon, her knife and flashlight lost in her fall, Dakota was defenseless. Death seemed certain.

Tyler dove into her, his arms wrapping around her waist like a safety punishing an airborne receiver. The landing would not be soft. She braced for it.

But Tyler twisted in the air, sacrificing his own body to cushion her fall. Dakota's weight crashed down on him, her elbow hitting something solid but the rest of her shielded from impact. Tyler had broken her fall and, by the sound of it, one or two of his ribs as well. He grunted, and it turned into a breathless wheeze.

Kinetic energy kept them rolling, a stroke of luck that popped Dakota back onto her feet.

Tyler did not get up so quickly. The leeches had him surrounded.

"Run!" he yelled. He grabbed a long, cylindrical object from the forest floor. It was a flashlight, no doubt dropped in their tumble.

Dakota planted her feet. "I'm not leaving you."

A greasy black circle formed around Tyler and slowly began closing in on him. The creatures seemed to be in no hurry to make their kill.

*Are they savoring it?*

Dakota forced herself to watch, to search for a way to help him. She couldn't leave him there to die. He hadn't left her.

"Run," Tyler repeated. Though his eyes darted frantically, searching for an escape, his tone was calm, almost brotherly, like the brother she had lost to him—*no, to those things*—six years ago. He flicked on the flashlight and spun full circle.

The leeches shrieked in unison. Those in the forefront scrambled over their kin to get away from the light.

Some dove toward Dakota.

"Run," Tyler said again. "I promise, I will be right behind you."

"I'm sorry," she mouthed. The creatures were nearly upon her. Without any light to guide her, she ran, her thoughts as dark as the woods that trapped her.

But not for long. Dakota sped into a break in the trees. Her eyes adjusted to the moonlight. She had found the trail, and she took off down it.

"Come on," Merwin's gravelly voice broke the silence ahead. A car's engine sputtered. "Turn, goddamn it."

"Merwin." Dakota ran up to the beat-up Chevy Malibu. "Thank God you're alive."

Merwin nodded. His eyes softened for a moment, then he

fixed his jaw. "Neither of us will be much longer if I don't get this car started."

He turned the engine again. The Malibu burst to life.

"Tyler?" he asked.

Dakota shook her head.

"Get in," he said.

"Wait for me," Tyler called, shooting from the woods and quickly covering the distance.

"Tyler!" Dakota couldn't believe her eyes. He was alive. How had he gotten away from them all?

The answer was simple—he hadn't. Her celebration had come prematurely. She gasped at the sight of what followed at Tyler's heels. With the help of the stars, she could see more of the leech monsters than she had imagined possible. They filed after one another like lemmings, the leader of the pack constantly changing.

No, Tyler was their leader. They were all, every one of them, following him.

"Hurry!" Dakota shouted. She ran around the car, opened the passenger side door, and climbed into the back seat, leaving the door open behind her. Merwin sat behind the wheel. Tyler barreled into the front end of the car.

As if it were the cue he had been waiting for, Merwin clicked on the lights then the high beams. The avalanche rolling toward them parted like the Red Sea around the car. Merwin yanked the stick shift into reverse and slammed on the gas.

"Stop," Dakota commanded, shaking Merwin's shoulder. "He's not in yet."

"Just giving us a little lead time, darling. He'll make it."

Merwin was right. Tyler sprinted around the open door and dove in as the car's speed continued to rise. A leech attached itself to Tyler, its tail spreading like feces across the sole of his sneaker. Its head flopped outside the car. Tyler crushed it with the door as he slammed it shut. The creature burst like a balloon filled with sewage. Its black fluid spattered Tyler and the dashboard. The remains of the leech decomposed. All that remained was a dark stain on the carpet.

"Here. Take this." Merwin slung his rifle onto Tyler's lap.

"You watch the front. I'll watch the back. Dakota, you've got double duty, left and right."

Tyler took the gun in his hands. He faced forward, a sentry guarding over unlikely wards.

"I trust you still know how to use that."

Merwin's words were callous, though Dakota doubted he meant to sound that way. Tyler nodded, keeping his eyes away from Dakota. Yeah, the sting kept on stinging. She still hated guns and the people who fired them, but she hated those fucking things outside even more.

Shit pancakes rained down onto the car as if the night sky itself were shattering. Some bounced off and rolled away. Others clung. Scratching sounds came from the roof. Two black blobs smeared the front windshield.

Merwin steered with one hand, his body twisting so that he could see out the back window. He never flinched, no matter where the creatures' gurgling and screeching came from. The Malibu bounced, rocked, and chugged its way down the narrow path, Merwin showing the precision of a Formula One driver in keeping the car out of the trees.

Dakota glanced over her shoulder, thinking she could help guide Merwin, and what she saw to her right seized her attention. Several black globs, ranging from softballs to beach balls in size, rolled out of the woods like boulders caught in a landslide.

Merwin must have seen them, too. He slammed on the gas and bulldozed his way through them. Some hit the fender and continued across the path. Others went under the car, making a rocky road even rockier. Still others ended up beneath the tires, squishing like rotten fruit beneath a mallet, which Dakota found the most satisfying. The sound brought her so much joy that she almost giggled.

*We may die tonight, but we're taking a shitload of them with us.*

The path was clear and widening. Dakota couldn't recall when exactly they had crossed into the camping area, but there they were. The parking lot wasn't much farther at the rate they were traveling.

Her gaze returned forward. All humor left her.

*Oh. My. God.*

A much bigger ball of slugs rolled toward them, a dark figure against a slightly less dark backdrop, matching speed with the Malibu just outside the range of its high beams. As it continued, other creatures joined the mass as if they were Play-Doh thrown hard enough to stick. They disappeared into the central mass, which grew bigger with every second.

"When we turn," Dakota said, "that thing is going to hit us."

"Then I will just have to drive us backward all the way down to Mexico." Merwin didn't turn to look. It was as if he could sense the evil forming in front of him and doubled his concentration on the road behind.

Dakota tapped the damaged rifle, still in Tyler's hands. "Why don't you give it a reason to think twice about following us?"

Tyler didn't respond. His gaze was lost inside that terrible ball. It was just as well. Dakota doubted that it was a good idea for any of them to open a window.

Then she saw what he was watching. The rolling ball was evolving, taking shape. A head, human in form, sprouted from the top as if it were the smallest sphere of a snowman. Shoulders came next, then arms. An upper torso rose from the black consortium. It reached out with oily fingers as if calling them home into its embrace.

Tyler sat still. His head seemed locked in place, his gaze fixed outside the front windshield. The monsters became a man, but not any man Dakota knew. A man with a wrecking ball for legs.

"Stop them," the doppelgänger hissed. "We hunger."

"Who is it talking to?" Dakota studied the figure. "Who is that?"

Tyler turned enough for Dakota to be able to make out the side of his face. He was crying. His knuckles were bone white as he gripped the rifle against his chest.

"My father," he whispered. He drove what remained of the butt of the rifle into Merwin's head.

# CHAPTER 20

Mark heard Abigail screaming outside, a few choice curse words directed his way, but he didn't feel the least bit sorry for her. She wasn't his responsibility. He hadn't told her to come out to the woods. He hadn't set those hunger-crazed nasties loose on everyone. He hadn't done shit.

*Fuck her.*

Besides, the party mobile belonged to Mark. Well, it was his dad's, anyway. That bitch could find her own place to hide.

Had she really thought he'd risk his own life to save hers? He'd have to be pretty damn stupid not to be afraid of something that was trying to eat him. Fear had made Mark close that camper door, and he wasn't ashamed to admit it, at least not to himself. He didn't want to die. He'd come to Galveston State Park to drink and trash his dad's motor home—and, when that other bitch, Dakota, had showed up, to get his dick wet. He had not gone there to have slugs eat him.

The night had started out so well. Mark had done a great job of getting himself liquored up. And he had cornered Dakota. The "fuck" part of his plan had been there for the taking. She didn't want to at first, but that never stopped him. Bitches always spread their legs eventually.

Then somehow, Mark's best-laid plans had fallen apart, and he'd gone from having a good fuck to getting fucked in the ass faster than his boner could deflate. He considered opening the door. The mature woman outside would likely throw herself all over him, forever grateful to Mark, her savior. Grieving the loss of her husband, she'd seek comfort in any way she could. She'd practically beg for Mark's cock.

But that would mean opening the door. The shrieking

outside was growing closer. The bitch wasn't worth it. He removed his finger from the latch and counted Abigail dead. Mark did wish her good speed, though. The faster Abigail ran, the farther she'd lead those things away from him.

*Good luck.*

He laughed then sobered as he concentrated on his own predicament. "Why aren't the fucking lights on, you fucking moron?" He hit the switch by the door. Nothing happened.

He growled. "Turn on the goddamn lamp." As much as he wanted to hit Luc, getting the lights on was Mark's first priority.

A desk lamp rested on a small table at the end of the sofa bed. Luc sat in the way, huddled on the floor with his knees tucked against his chest. He rocked back and forth. "I didn't mean to leave you," he murmured. "I was scared. I didn't know what else to do."

"Who the fuck are you talking to?" Mark kicked his friend in his ribs. "Get a grip, man. Bo's dead, and we will be, too, if you don't get the fuck out of my way."

Luc didn't seem to notice. He continued to sway, muttering something to his dead brother.

The woods outside sounded alive, electric. As always, Mark had to take matters into his own hands. He cursed his useless frat mate under his breath. Luc was lost to the world, lost within himself. *Fuck him.*

Mark shoved his way past Luc and seized the lamp, tore off its lampshade, and tossed it aside. He smiled as his fingers turned the small black switch. It clicked, but the light bulb remained unlit.

*It's not plugged in.* Mark grabbed the cord and pulled it out from behind the table. As he ran his fingers along the thin wire, it wasn't long before he found the problem.

"What the fuck?" Mark stared down at the damaged wire, whose plug end was missing entirely. Shrieking, gurgling, and hissing came from outside. Luc moaned in response. Mark threw his hand against the wall, screaming out his frustration and fear.

*The halogen!* A giant camping lantern sat along the back wall of the camper. It was shaped like a bucket and had a metal handle that swung over the cover and cylindrical bulb. Mark lifted it off the floor. It went from heavy to light in less than a second as its rechargeable battery fell to the floor. The bottom of the light was missing. Its insides were chewed to bits. Black slime covered Mark's hand.

He threw the lantern against the wall. Something skittered away from where it landed.

"Fuck!" Mark stumbled backward. He squealed in terror as he collided with something solid and alive behind him. It was Luc, who was standing now and had broken his fall.

"Get out your flashlight," Mark said, turning back to where he had spotted movement only a moment before. He saw nothing. He didn't hear anything, either. The ugly, unnatural sounds emanating from the creatures outside had stopped.

*They're inside.* Mark fumbled in his jacket's inner pocket, his fingers at last curling around the flashlight he'd claimed from Dakota after he had tripped her. The flashlight didn't go on when his thumb clicked the button. Mark shook it, and it rattled strangely. *Damned thing better not be broken.* Maybe it had loosened in its fall. Fighting off panic, he twisted the top on tight and tried the switch again. The flashlight came to life.

He aimed it at the floor. Shallow black puddles rose shrieking from the corner. They slithered through a hole in the floorboard and were gone. The suckers had scratched or eaten their way through the Winnebago's frame.

Mark trembled. He stepped back onto Luc's toes. The big man didn't budge.

When Mark turned to face him, his flashlight following, a huge slithering mass rose high above Luc's head. The leech's mouth was exposed, and in it was half of Luc's cheek. It gurgled and squirmed like a hypnotized cobra, spattering blood everywhere as its tail coiled tighter around the young man's neck.

Luc's eyes were open wide, and Mark could still see life in them. The big man's stare was lost, hopeless, the look of someone who knew his death was upon him. Luc's arms rose. They grasped at air, groped Mark's jacket. Luc's expression begged for help, but Mark had none to give. He planted his heel in Luc's gut and pushed him back. Then he shined his light directly at the thing around Luc's neck.

The screech the creature emitted was loud enough to burst Mark's eardrums. Still, he kept the flashlight pointed exactly where he needed it to be. If that leech thing even had the slightest opening, Mark knew he'd be a goner.

The monster made its move. It spiraled down Luc toward the floor, thrashing and eating trenches into Luc's body as it went, severing his right arm at the elbow. Blood sprayed in all directions. It hit Mark, covering him in dark-red blotches that reminded him of that asshole who made millions by throwing paint at a white canvas.

At Luc's feet, the giant leech detached all but a narrow coil that was wrapped around his ankle. Luc's head snapped back like a Pez dispenser, the front half of his neck no longer where it was supposed to be. He fell atop himself, dead, nearly bringing Mark down with him.

The creature exploded like a mushroom cloud underneath the sofa bed, dragging Luc with it. Luc's body was far too big to fit under there. It jammed up at the thigh, but the thing tugging it just kept eating Luc shorter and shorter.

Mark hopped over his friend's remains and slid, he hoped, out of that big fucker's reach. His light bounced around the camper as he moved. A small leech fell from the wall above the couch and slid under it to join in the feast. Two more scurried in from somewhere in the back of the camper, inches from where he had just been.

Startled by their sudden movement, Mark scampered like a crab on palms and heels, never looking behind him to see where he was heading or what might be waiting. Fear of the three-footer made him keep his eyes on the sofa. He could hear the creatures feeding, slurping. By then, the things had crammed most of Luc beneath it with them.

Mark's back hit the dividing wall between the cab and living area. The leeches could be anywhere. Those bloodsuckers could climb. They could be close—on the walls nearby, on the ceiling above.

The flashlight shook in Mark's hands. He chewed the inside

of his mouth until he tasted blood. He couldn't bring himself to look up. How could he take his eyes off that thing under the sofa? He knew it was watching him. It wanted him next.

Desperate, Mark wished someone else would save him. He didn't want to be in control anymore. He sure as hell didn't feel in control anymore. Why couldn't someone show up and help him?

With quick jerks intended to catch any slinking slugs off guard, Mark danced his flashlight's beam across every wall. The ceiling was harder. The image of those nasty bastards hanging above him, gurgling mud-thick drool, rusted what little remained of Mark's steel.

But he had to look. He took in a deep breath and glanced up. *Nothing.* Mark exhaled.

A bang came at the door, then another. More came from the outside walls. Mark covered his head with his hands. *The light! I have to keep the light on them.*

It sounded like some dickheads were throwing four-pound cow patties at the camper, something he might have done under different circumstances. Only these patties didn't slide off the walls. They crawled and scratched, digging in with their poisonous spines.

The vehicle rocked on its axles as the pounding grew harder, more frequent. Scratching and gurgling came from above, below, and everywhere in between.

"Come out, Mark," a voice said from outside the camper.

*Frosh?* It couldn't be him out there. The voice was an exact match. Well, not really. Frosh didn't have a voice. Frosh was dead.

*Maybe that bitch hearing her dead husband's voice wasn't crazy after all. Or maybe I'm going crazy along with her.*

*Come join our fraternity,* a voice not his own beckoned from inside his mind.

Mark pushed at his temples with the flats of his palms. "Get out of my head, you fucker. You're not Frosh. I'm not stupid enough to fall for your tricks."

*Join us,* the voice that belonged to Frosh but was not Frosh commanded.

"You let me die, Mark," Bo's voice sounded from outside the camper. "Why did you let us die, Mark? All for a piece of tail?"

Mark didn't answer. He had enough wits left to know the creature was either taunting him or trying to provoke him. The voices were not his frat mates. His college buddies were dead, every last one of them.

Mark was not setting foot outside that trailer.

*Was she worth all this, Mark?* The voice was Luc's this time. Though it sounded like Bo's, Luc's voice always had a little more swagger to it, like he thought he was the shit even though he came second. *Look at me, Mark.*

Mark looked.

All except the top three-quarters of Luc's head had been drawn beneath the sofa bed. His upper teeth had caught against the frame of the dual-purpose furniture. Mark could see their surrounding gum area and even some cheekbone, where that big fucker had stripped off Luc's flesh. Luc's head tilted onto the top of his scalp. His eyes rolled back slightly in their sockets. They were cold and glassy, like marbles, and stared right at Mark.

Mark shined the flashlight on him, and Luc's head disappeared forever beneath the sofa bed.

"It's all good here, Mark," the Bo mimic said outside. "We live forever now. Join us."

*Join us,* Luc and Frosh's voices said in unison. Scratching amplified around Mark, and the voices in his head ramped up with it. Together, they scratched away at Mark's sanity.

"Join us," the Bo thing repeated.

"Go fuck yourself!" Mark shouted.

A loud crash shook the door in its frame. A second thud dented the metal as if it were tin foil. A third hit came and retreated with the door itself.

"Fuck!" Mark scurried along the wall, away from the open doorway. His hand plopped into something wet, and he screamed. Shining the light on what he had touched, he saw an overturned beer can.

Mark turned and pointed his flashlight outside. A shadowy mass, shaped like Bo but fluid, dragged what remained of the door away with what appeared to be a twelve-foot-long human arm. As the light fell upon the Bo-like figure, it dissolved into dozens of balloon-sized teardrops splashing onto the ground. The many puzzle pieces that had once fit together into a common form—a cohesive unit, a *collective*—scattered, shrinking away from the light.

"I see you, Bo," Mark called at the fleeing creatures. He laughed hysterically. "Now, where's the pledge?"

"Join us." Frosh's voice came from off to the right. Mark turned toward it just in time to see a twisting vine of worms emerging from a humanoid dark mass, growing like that famous beanstalk. It came toward him fast, but not fast enough. Mark's laughter turned into frantic babbling as his light hit the tentacle-like formation, whose component parts burst off like corn kernels in a popper.

He stood and stabbed his flashlight toward the sofa bed, a warning to what hid beneath that it best not come out, then approached the doorway, waving the flashlight as if he were staging a performance and each one of those slug fucks was its star. They scattered, their shrieks a symphony to Mark's ears.

"You can't have me," he yelled. "You hear me? You can't have—"

"Join us." Luc's voice came from above, cutting short Mark's tirade.

The light flickered and died. *No. Not the fucking battery.* Mark shook the flashlight and flicked the switch, but nothing happened. His arms and legs flailed as a slimy wet worm latched onto his face and lifted him into the air. Another leech tied itself around his left arm, a third around his right. The flashlight fell from Mark's trembling hand.

A leech slid into his throat, stifling his screams, but he screamed anew when it slid into his stomach. *Join us*, the voices—Luc, Bo, Frosh, and so many others—chanted loudly, tapping directly into his brain. The creatures hoisted him up onto the camper's roof, where the real screaming began.

# CHAPTER 21

His father's voice had been constantly in his mind since he'd left the cellar. It asked him, then told him, then begged him to destroy that light. It kept poking and prodding at his psyche, making him squirm, making him want to scream so he could drown out good ol' Dad if only for a moment. If Charlie hadn't destroyed the lantern, Tyler would have done it just to make his father shut up.

Now he knew it wouldn't have worked. Even after *they* had gotten what they wanted and everyone was scrambling into the night, they pressed Tyler for more assistance, pushed him toward breaking. Yet he defied them and ignored the debt he owed them, holding steady for Dakota's sake and for Charlie's.

The leech creatures had come to collect, and they would take what they wanted, with him or from him. They had started with Charlie.

*Why? You didn't have to take him. He was my friend.*

Tyler fought with the voices in his head—so many voices, yet they all sounded like his father: quiet and full of hate. Like Tyler.

*We're your friends, Tyler. We saved you. We cared for you. We raised you. Remember.*

Tyler felt the weight of the gun in his hands. He hadn't held a rifle since that day he shot Dakota's brother. The feel of its smooth wooden stock, its cold metal barrel, reminded him of all the awful things he had done.

He did remember. How could he ever forget? Even as Merwin drove them out of the park, still futilely believing they had a chance, Tyler's mind was sucked back to a day long before he'd shot Stevie Coogan, back when he'd first learned to shoot.

"That's it," his father whispered into his ear. Hot breath sizzled down the nape of Tyler's neck. His father's nose tickled his hair. Tyler shivered. He cringed every time Daddy got that close. "Release your breath before you shoot. Make sure your arm is calm and still... steady. Don't you miss, now, boy."

*Calm and still.* The deer looked calm and still as it drank from the lake. The water was calm and still, too. Tyler couldn't be that way, not when his father stood so close. He knew too well what would happen if he missed. Daddy wouldn't like that. Daddy wouldn't like that one bit.

"Aim. Breathe. Shoot," his father instructed.

Tyler aimed as well as a frail eight-year-old could, holding a rifle that weighed half as much as he did and stretched twice as long as his arms. The deer came in and out of his sight as the barrel swayed up and down. He would have to time the shot with the sway, the rifle dancing to the rhythm of his heart.

"Shoot the damn thing before it runs off," Father whispered between clenched teeth.

"I don't wanna kill—"

"You kill it, or I'm gonna kill you."

The tears forming in Tyler's eyes made aiming that much harder. He didn't want to hurt the deer. It hadn't done anything to him, but he was terrified to face what would happen if he missed the shot, or worse, failed to shoot at all. He aimed. He breathed. He fired.

He missed.

The recoil jarred him in the shoulder. Tyler stumbled backward and tripped, falling on his buttocks. *Oh no.* His body trembled. Where the deer had been, only reeds and water remained. *Oh, please, no.*

"You worthless, good-for-nothing little snot." His father's shadow loomed over him. Tyler began to snivel. He couldn't look up, couldn't face the man or the punishment he knew was coming. He raised his head just high enough to see his father's belt buckle, a fat silver rectangular depiction of the Confederate flag. He had seen it many times before.

Too many times.

"I oughta beat you black and blue. That buck could have fed us for a week."

"I'm sorry, Daddy." Tyler stumbled over the words. His lips were quivering. Tears ran down his cheeks. Why was he always screwing up? The broken bones were bad enough. The other stuff was worse.

"*Sorry* don't put no food on the table, shit for brains." His father unbuckled his belt. "Now, how are you gonna make it right, boy?"

Tyler scrambled backward, dragging the rifle with him. "No, Daddy. I'll make it right, I promise. I'll find a new deer." He ejected the fired cartridge case like Daddy had taught him then closed the bolt to chamber the next bullet. "Next time, I'm gonna shoot it good, I swear."

"It's too late for that, boy. There's only one way to make it right now." Tyler's father pulled off his belt and folded it in his hand. He unbuttoned his jeans. Tyler began to sob.

"No, Daddy. I don't want to," he said between sniffles. Snot trickled from his nose. The gun trembled in his hands.

"You don't get to tell me 'no,' boy."

Tyler scurried backward on hands and heels. "I won't," he shouted, nearly hysterical. "I-I wish you were dead!"

"What did you say to me, boy?" His father whipped his belt buckle across Tyler's jaw. Tyler rolled with the hit but immediately tasted blood.

"I was just gonna make you use your mouth, but now you've gone and made me bloody it." His father crouched and reached for him. Tyler retreated farther. A reed tickled his ear. His hands sank into mud and water.

"Come here."

"No, Daddy. Please!" Tyler kicked at his hands, but his father grabbed him by the ankle.

"You're only making it worse for yourself, boy."

Tyler flopped onto his back as his father dragged him closer. He didn't know how, but the rifle fired.

His father's eyes burst open. Tyler saw pain and confusion in them.

"I'm sorry, Daddy," he said, gaining his feet. "I... I... I didn't mean to."

His father's face looked strained, as if he were struggling for a bowel movement that wouldn't come. His hands covered his stomach. Dark blood seeped through his fingers. He let go with his right hand and reached for Tyler. He staggered forward, lunged at Tyler, but fell into the shallows, and his son easily scooted out of the way.

Tyler had seen Daddy floundering like that before, usually after he drank his special drink that Tyler was never allowed to have. His father was always at his worst then but also easiest to avoid. Except when Tyler was in bed, and his father stumbled like that into his room after Mommy started snoring. Sometimes, Tyler hid under the bed or in the closet, but Daddy always found him.

Daddy stumbled past him this time, right into the water. He was hurt. Tyler knew he was going to be in so much trouble when his father got up. He cried and cried. He would have to do so much to make it right.

His father's face was underwater. He sputtered, his hand twitching erratically at the surface, splashing and sending ripples across the lake. He lurched out of the water, gasping and coughing, only to fall face-first back into it. His body shook as if he were being electrocuted. The spasms slowed, then stopped.

"Daddy?" Tyler approached cautiously. "Daddy?" he called again, poking his father's leg with the end of the barrel. He jumped back, expecting his father to spring on him, but the man stayed down.

"Daddy? Are you dead?" Tyler knew it was a stupid question. *Dead guys don't talk, you dummy.* How many times had he wished his father would die? He had never dared to say it aloud, fearing that no matter where his father was, he'd somehow hear the curse. Now, after it finally slipped from his mouth, his father lay face down and motionless in the water. He wished he could take it back, fearing that his father would still find a way to punish him for what he'd said and done.

The lake began to bubble as if God were blowing into it through a giant straw. The bubbling turned into boiling. Tyler took a few hesitant steps backward, his eyes transfixed on the air pockets popping on the surface. They were coming closer.

The water darkened. It looked as if an oil leak had sprung somewhere in the lakebed. It made the air feel heavy, taste stale, and smell foul. Something evil was in that water. Something darker than oil, gushing like a geyser from some unseen chasm, tainted the water with its corruption. The pristine lake rotted before Tyler's feet.

His father began to move. At first, Tyler thought he was floating, but that didn't make any sense, not in only a few inches of water. Then the body jerked forward, skimming across the water. His father looked as though he had fallen while waterskiing and refused to let go of the rope. Something was pulling him out deeper. When he reached the center of the lake, whatever had hold of him dragged him under.

The water bubbled fiercely then, as if a school of piranhas had gone on a feeding frenzy.

"Never hurt you... again... Tyler. No one... tell. No one... ever know."

Tyler gasped. His body tensed, locked in fear. He only managed to turn his head, looking everywhere for the speaker, the person who had witnessed his terrible crime. No one was there. The voice seemed to rise out of the lake itself. Maybe he'd called it somehow with his wish that had come true. Was it the voice of whatever had taken his father's body? It had told him he'd be safe—and yet it frightened him.

Whatever it was, something had awakened in the depths of that lake. Something that knew his name.

A shadow formed beneath the surface, spread thin through the water, then closed in on itself, concentrating into a thick black mushroom that looked as if it would sprout its way into the sky. It rose higher and took form, reminding Tyler of Jesus, who could walk on water, as his mother had told him. Was this Jesus, rising from the grave to pass judgment on the guilty?

Tyler's teeth chattered. He wanted so badly to run, but his legs refused to cooperate. He couldn't look away. Jesus, or whoever the black mushroom hid, had a power over Tyler that fixed his feet to the dirt on which they stood.

It didn't look like any picture of Jesus that Tyler had ever seen, and it didn't rise out of the water. It stayed just below the surface, just beyond the reach of the sunlight, in that hazy gray layer where all light died. Tyler could make out a shape, even enough details to call it a face. It resembled his father, a looming figure in the dark who wanted to hurt Tyler, to punish him for being bad. And in Daddy's eyes, he was always bad even when he wasn't sure how.

*It's okay, buddy.*

The figure spoke, or at least Tyler thought it was the figure. The voice was inside his head. He shrank away from it. His father had already come back to haunt him.

*I've treated you so badly, little buddy. But no more, okay? Don't be afraid. I won't hurt you.*

"But I shot you."

*It's okay, Tyler. I know you didn't mean to. Besides, I'm better now. It's so much better in here.*

"In the lake?"

*Yes. In the lake, in this forest. This should be our home now. We should live here, you and me. I can be a good father to you now. No more pain. No more hurting. And we can be friends, too. You'll see.*

"You're not going to punish me?"

*Never again, buddy. You and I are gonna be the best of friends.*

"Friends?" Tyler didn't understand. The figure in the water sounded like his father, but he knew it couldn't be him. His father was dead, and Tyler was responsible. He crossed his arms and held himself close. Maybe it really was the ghost of his father, come back from the dead to fetch his son. *Please don't hurt me, Daddy.*

*I won't, buddy. We're friends now, and friends don't hurt friends. Ain't you never had a friend before?*

Tyler's face reddened. He was ashamed to admit the answer to that question, and if that voice really belonged to his father, its owner would know that Tyler rarely left the house except on Dad's "camping getaways," which usually ended with Tyler barely able to walk. Truth was, he'd never wanted to have friends before. Friends did things together, had sleepovers. Any friends of Tyler would have had to meet his father sooner or later.

And then there would be no more friends.

"You're not my father. Who... what are you?"

*Does it matter? I'm your friend, and I could be your father. I got rid of the bad one for you. No one has to know he's dead. No one ever has to know you killed him.* The figure burst like a star after imploding, unidentifiable masses winding like river otters, swimming off in all directions. As quickly as they had sped away, they regathered into a central mass.

"We are all friends," a dozen voices said, mostly in unison, twanging like the dying tones of a cymbal. None of them belonged to his father.

"Where's my dad?" Tyler asked, his voice breaking. Tears ran down his face.

*Don't cry, buddy,* his father's voice said. *I'm down here. It's so nice down here, so many friends. This is my home now. But you can come back and see me anytime. And if you come at night, we can talk and play games, and I can show you all the neat things I can do. You're going to be a good boy and come back and see me, won't you, Tyler?*

Tyler nodded, though he didn't mean it.

*You run along now, buddy. And whenever you get lonely, just remember you got all your pals here waiting for you at the lake.*

"I... I can go now?"

*Of course, Tyler. But please do come back. We'll... I'll miss you if you don't.*

Tyler felt the strength return to his limbs and was able to move again. He backed away from the water, his eyes fixed on the form beneath it. The figure watched him back. It looked like it was waving.

*Oh, and one more thing, buddy. When people ask—and they will ask—you tell them your daddy went off with some woman. Just got in the car with her and left. Don't tell them anything else, buddy. If you do, they'll know you killed him. You don't want them to know that, do you? They'll hurt you worse than your father did. Lock you up someplace where you'll never be found.*

*So remember, Daddy left with a woman. They'll figure out the rest. You can't tell anyone about your new friends, okay, buddy?*

Tyler nodded.

*You promise?*

"I promise," Tyler whispered. That promise he intended to keep. He wanted to forget everything that had happened that day, and he never, ever, wanted anyone to know what he had done to his father.

Someone remembered, though. The things in the water knew.

His hands were hurting. He looked down and was surprised to see the rifle still in them, his knuckles bloodless from holding it so tightly.

He turned and ran, sprinting all the way back to the park's entrance where he then wandered in a daze until the cops came and got him after someone apparently had called them about an unsupervised child with a rifle. As the police drove him away from the park, Tyler swore he'd never return.


But he had returned the next summer. Alone, friendless, and with no one to talk to but his mother, who spent most of her time in a drunken stupor, Tyler might have raised himself if not for the friends he had made by the lake. He hopped on his bike and rode down to the park eleven miles away just to have someone to talk to, someone who wanted to play. At first, he would only stay the night, but the occasional soiree turned into longer visits, sometimes three or four days at a time. His mother never seemed to notice or care that he was missing.

As the years went by, he camped there, lived there, learned how to hunt and kill like his father had always wanted him to. He had found a better teacher. A better father.

It took a few more years for Tyler to admit to himself what the creatures wanted in return and why they had even befriended him in the first place. At that point, it was too late to get out. They were all he had.

When Tyler was twelve, he brought a boy he had met in the campgrounds down to meet his friends, though the boy never knew that was his purpose. They had skipped rocks across the lake and, when night came, had spread out their sleeping bags and connected dots in the sky until they fell asleep. When Tyler awoke the next morning, the boy was gone, but his sleeping bag remained. The evening that followed, his lake friends multiplied.

He had always sort of known what the creatures wanted from him, but they had never tried to take it from him. Tyler had been their link to the human world. They had been his escape from it.

That boy he had skipped rocks with was the first. How many unwitting souls had he led to that cursed place since? How many innocents had he made food for worms? More than a handful. In eight years, only Stevie Coogan had come close to getting away, and he might have succeeded if Tyler hadn't stopped him. The sun had risen. All that stood between Coogan and safety was Tyler's rifle. On that day, Tyler learned the hardest lesson either father had ever taught him: it was one thing to lure a person to his death and something else entirely to kill him.

Sure, Tyler had only delivered the finishing touches, but that fact did nothing to lesson his guilt. And when he saw the impact of his actions in the eyes of that teenage girl in pigtails, how he had single-handedly destroyed her life, he realized he had become the real monster—a different breed from what his father had been, or even his friends in the lake, but a monster all the same.

"Stop them," the things pretending to be Tyler's father hissed outside the car. They would not be quiet. They would never be quiet, unless...

*Unless I give them what they want.*

"We hunger."

Tyler had gone out to Galveston State Park earlier that day to find closure, to put an end to his guilt. Was he such a coward, so afraid of being alone and dying alone, that he would find himself helping them again? He had spent six years alone, for Christ's sake. Where were his "friends" then?

Tears rolled down Tyler's face, as they had the day he first met the creatures. *Maybe I'll give them just the one.*

"Who is it talking to? Who is that?" Dakota asked, leaning forward in her seat.

"My father." Tyler shut out the voices by bashing Merwin in the skull with his own rifle.

Surprise flashed across Dakota's face before she covered it to protect herself, but Tyler saw her expression long enough to realize he had wronged her again. The car swerved off the trail. Merwin was out cold behind the wheel. The car smashed into a tree. Metal bent. Glass shattered.

Tyler was thrown forward. He hit his head on the dashboard. With blurred eyes, he fumbled for the door latch.

The back door opened before he could open his. By the time Tyler could stumble out of the car, Dakota was dashing down the trail. He blinked his vision clear and raised the rifle.

"Shoot her." The creature, still half Tyler's father and half revolving mound of blood-sucking monstrosities, rolled across the hood of the car, avoiding the still-functioning headlights. It moved beside Tyler, sending several of its component parts after Dakota.

Tyler aimed. He breathed. He pulled the trigger.

Dakota ran on. The bullet hit a tree more than a few feet away. Tyler had missed on purpose.

"Again," the creatures shouted.

"No. I won't."

"She's escaping. She'll tell."

"I shot her damn brother for you, kept your dirty little secret even after it got me sent to prison for six years. Our dirty little secret. I deserved what I got. She didn't. I destroyed her life. I won't destroy her as well."

Tyler threw the rifle on the ground. For the first time in his life, he stared his father right in the eye.

"Not her?" the voices asked, some high, some low, no longer in unison. Creature upon creature piled over one another, bearing mouths and spines, shapeless but ever in motion. "Not her!" they shrieked. "Not her—then you!"

Dakota disappeared beyond Tyler's sight as his friends

swarmed over him. He heard a scream, full of dread and anguish, and a moment passed before he realized it was his own.

# CHAPTER 22

I should have killed him. I should have killed him. I should have killed him.

"I mean, what in the fuck was that?" Dakota wanted to howl, but she could hear the leeches pounding after her. The last thing she needed was to announce her location. She might as well have shouted, "Dinner's ready!"

*I knew there was something wrong with that boy.* She had always known it. A fucked-up night from hell and an army of ravenous bloodsuckers had somehow clouded her judgment.

It was still clouded. *Think, girl,* she scolded herself. *You're not out of the woods yet.* The appropriateness of the expression almost made her laugh. She was close to being out of the real woods, but as for being out trouble, she had a long way to go. The creatures were gaining.

The grass whispered behind her. Any moment now, one of those ugly fuckers would latch onto her back or tie up her feet. Though she trembled on the inside, she ran with confidence, her mind always on the ultimate goal. The ground beneath her feet grew firmer, the dirt packed by frequent travel. After a few more steps, she hit pavement.

Her car sat in the parking lot, looking unharmed. Dakota dared to hope, until she remembered that her keys had been in her duffle bag, the contents of which Bo had dumped onto the cabin floor. She veered away from the car and headed toward the ranger station. *Please, let it be unlocked.* There was no place else to go.

The light coming from the station was angelic, calling her. Like a drowning woman seeing the shore, Dakota craved that light.

But she still had the expanse of the lot to cross, while a wave of leeches rolled closer. Dakota's heel-to-toe strides bounced her like a gazelle toward the building's front steps. She heard nothing behind her, but the forest to her left erupted. Branches snapped with crisp, clean breaks. Trees creaked, then crackled, before falling with a boom. Everywhere, leaves rustled as if caught in a hurricane.

Monsters sprang from the brush.

Dakota hurdled up the stairs and raced to the door. She turned the knob, only to find the door locked. She battered it with her palms, threw her shoulder into it, but the door didn't budge, and no one answered it. To her left, leeches flung themselves onto the building, smacking into the wood and sticking to it. Some dropped onto the landing.

With a panicked cry, she circled the deck to her right and turned the corner. The structure sat between her and the woods, but all that meant was that she wouldn't see the creatures coming. Her fingers trailed along the wall until they came to a window.

"Open!" Dakota shouted as she slid her hands upward along the panes. The window was locked, but she knew how to fix that. Shards of glass rained onto her sneakers. Some dug into the elbow she had used to smash the pane. She shoved her hand through the hole in the glass, jagged stalagmites stabbing at her skin, and reached for the latches. Her nose mushed against the window as she stretched up to its top. One lock came undone, then the second. She pulled her arm out, pushed open the window, and climbed inside just as a leech cannonballed past her head.

She closed the window behind her, though she knew it wouldn't even slow the creatures down. Before she could take a step away from it, the lights flickered. Then they went out.

A rumbling started outside, and the lights came back on but only at a fraction of their former strength. They gave the interior a copper tint. Dakota feared they would not be bright enough to stop the creatures.

Pounding came from everywhere as if a battalion of archers had shot their payload into the station. Dakota looked around for an idea, a weapon, anything. Instead, she found herself standing empty-handed and panicking in the middle of a welcome station filled with only a desk, some chairs, a counter, an ancient-looking statue of Smokey Bear, and a ton of tourism pamphlets touting all the great fun the park had to offer.

*Fuck this park, fuck those brochures, and fuck you, Smokey.*

The gold placard on the door behind the counter caught her eye. Employees Only.

*I'm sure Merwin won't mind.* She hopped onto the counter and slid over to the other side. *Merwin.* Dakota shuddered. She had left him back there to be devoured. The car had crashed, and she had reacted, unthinking, survival instincts taking over. Though she knew there was nothing she could have done, it didn't make her feel any better about leaving him.

*That other one, though... I hope they tear that fucker to shreds.* Tyler's betrayal, right when she had finally found it in her heart to forgive him, still stung, and her foolishness for letting him gain her trust stung even more.

The sound of glass breaking set a fire under her feet. *They're inside.* She tried the door and found it locked, so she kicked it open and entered what looked like a break area. She slammed the door shut and knocked over some nearby storage shelves to block it. *It won't hold them off for long.* When she saw the window on the far wall, she doubted the blockade would hold them off at all.

The room spread out like a studio apartment. To her left was a full-service kitchen, complete with a large refrigerator and a four-burner stove. In front of her and to her right was an employee lounge.

A plan began to form. *It always works in the movies.* She ran to the refrigerator. She opened the door and began ripping the shelves out and tossing them and their contents onto the floor. A jar of pickles rolled under the counter. A carton of eggs somehow held together, but yolk oozed out through its cracks. Water bottles, cans of soda, deli meat, condiments, and a host of mystery dishes hidden in Tupperware containers littered the floor.

After scooping out the remaining produce with her foot, Dakota examined her handiwork. *Looks kind of cramped, but it should do.* She smiled. A loud whack against the door, followed by the sound of wood splintering, ended her self-congratulating. She turned and found exactly what she was looking for: a knife block. She drew the biggest blade from it, a six-inch beast that looked as if it could dice brick. Then she headed to the stove.

*If the entire cast of* Expendables *can do this, so can you,* Dakota reasoned. *Just turn on the gas, cut the tube, light something on fire, and boom, everything goes bye-bye.* The ranger station would be blown to hell while she hid safely in the refrigerator. She just hoped the fire wouldn't burn out all her oxygen, but she had no time for second-guessing.

She turned all the knobs on the front of the stove then looked down at the burners. Electric, not gas.

"Fuck! Goddamn piece of shit!"

She kicked the appliance so hard the oven racks rattled. Now what? How could she escape? A creature was burrowing its way through a growing crack in the building's door.

Dakota frantically opened cabinets and sifted through drawers, looking for a means to fight, a means to survive. Frustrated, she threw a can of corn at the slimy worm hanging through the door and hit it. A shriek rose from its gaping mouth, and it wriggled even faster. Dakota had only managed to piss it off.

*Chemicals?* Maybe she could burn the leeches with bleach or Pine-Sol or motherfucking Lemon Pledge. She tore open the doors beneath the sink and saw nothing but a six-pack of paper towels.

She pulled it out and howled, her arms lifting it over her head, ready to throw it in frustration, then stopped. *If I can't blow the place up, maybe I can still burn it down.* She slammed the package of paper towels onto the counter and tore it open. Carrying a roll in each hand to the stovetop, she thanked the heavens she had already turned the burners on. Outside, the generator bucked like an old lawn mower, and the lights flickered. She wondered if it had enough juice left to power up the range.

She pressed a roll against the burner. Smoke started to rise. *Come on.* Then the towels burned like a cigarette. Dakota was about to give up when the damn thing finally lit up.

"Fuck you, Smokey!" she yelled, laughing as she threw the paper towel roll at the door. It rolled itself out. Dakota stopped laughing. She waited until her second roll burst into flames before trying again. That one turned the piled-up pamphlets and dusty literature into a bonfire. The creature halfway through the door squealed and started working its way back to the other side as flames licked at its body.

It was too early to celebrate. Other cracks had since appeared in the door. Even as splinters crackled like kindling in the fire at one side of the door, the flames had not yet reached the other side and had little fodder to help them spread in that direction. The dim lighting didn't seem to discourage the creatures. Black, oozing masses squeezed through fissures like soft chocolate forced through a cheese grater. They shrieked and gargled, spitting and secreting their sludge onto the door panels. Only a thin barrier kept her from them and them from her, and that barrier was crumbling fast.

Dakota had to make the blaze bigger. She nearly stumbled over the vegetable oil. *Perfect.* As if God had sent her a message. She popped it open and squirted the curtains, the carpet, and the couch then the tip of her third paper towel roll. It flamed, and she threw it onto the couch.

The fire spread rapidly up the back of the couch and onto the drapes over the window. Dakota hadn't noticed that the window had been cracked open until the fire illuminated it. And that wasn't all the fire revealed. A small horde of leeches pushed through the crack, their midsections twisting like balloon animals. When the fire hit them, they shrieked in unison, unable to back away quickly enough. The fire caused something in them to boil. *Blood,* Dakota guessed. They swelled and burst like gorged ticks beneath a match.

That gave Dakota her first solid idea. One of the cupboards had someone's personal hygiene items in it, including hairspray. *Just like in the movies.*

After igniting her fourth flaming paper towel roll, she

used the aerosol can like a blowtorch, charring the door and exploding a half dozen leeches. Unlike her first movie-inspired trick, the hairspray worked, but it ran out quickly. The fire was spreading too slowly. While she battled with the creatures at the door, those still alive at the window got smarter. They propelled themselves through the glass.

Dakota dashed back behind the counter. The carpet and cabin wall were burning well now. Some of the slug things rolled in to find death. They popped like water balloons, black juices evaporating in the flames. Others, though, wiggled around the patches of fire.

They were moving in on her. With nowhere to go, Dakota's final stand had come.

She dumped most of the vegetable oil across the counter and, after lighting her last two rolls of paper towels, set it ablaze. Creatures bobbed and hissed behind a wall of flame. They shrieked and fled where the flames burned brightest. Dakota aimed to make the biggest, brightest fire those slimy fuckers had ever seen.

She doused the floor with what was left of the oil and stood one roll in it to burn. The other she rolled onto the carpet and added to the spreading flames and screeching worms.

They were dying. *Some of them at least.*

Dakota coughed. Her eyes stung. The fire, growing tall and strong, was feeding off the very air she needed to breathe. In spite of the danger, a sense of pride washed over her. She'd die by her own hand before those squirming hell spawn could feed on her.

She grabbed the kitchen knife and curled up inside the damp refrigerator. Smoke swallowed the ceiling. She found herself wondering if she'd suffocate or burn. Whatever her fate, she resigned herself to it so long as the creatures never got their fill.

In another room, a smoke detector raised its alarm. Dakota closed the door, shutting herself into the darkness as the leeches pressed closer and the fire raged on.

# CHAPTER 23

*Morning*

The sun rose over Galveston State Park, its face beaming brightly, unaffected by the events that had transpired while it slept. Abigail had never seen a finer sight.

Of those who had shared a night in hell with her, she alone seemed to have survived. She'd only witnessed a handful of deaths, her husband's among them, but she had to conclude the worst for them all, even if she hoped otherwise. If any others had survived, she assumed that like her, they now had a greater appreciation for all that was light and good in a world so terribly out of balance.

Even the swirling reds, blues, and whites of the police and emergency vehicles—a procession of noisy, epilepsy-inducing strobes—were beautiful to her eyes, and their light was but a sliver of the sun's brilliance. The police officers were her protectors, but the sun was her savior.

She hadn't told them much, only what she knew they would believe. People were dying. She had seen a few murders and suspected several more. Her husband had been taken from her by a vicious killer, which she couldn't describe because *it* kept to the dark. Four were dead, she told them—two boys from the local college, a parole officer, and her husband. Others had been hunted in the dark and were lost in the woods.

What else could she tell them? They would have to see those creatures themselves before they'd believe in monsters. Even as the officer examined her back—stinging, ruined flesh, raw and exposed—Abigail knew the truth would not satisfy him. Instead, she told them the half-truths that would get them moving—not giving them much information at all.

A young man had found her twelve miles from the park's entrance, still running, her pace snail slow but her mind unwilling to relent. She had told that young man the truth, every bit of it. He looked at her as though she were crazy and dropped her off at the nearest police station without a word. As soon as she was out of his car, he drove away.

Even without a description of the killer or killers, Abigail had told a wild story. Frenzied panic still ran through her, and her eyes watched every corner, waiting for shadows to spring from shadows. The policemen seemed ready to dismiss her as some jonesing junkie until one of them noticed her back. Their speculation as to what might have caused the wounds—they talked to each other in front of her as if she wasn't right there— might have amused Abigail had she any capacity for amusement left.

"A cleat," one had said, a conclusion that the others had solemnly approved as fabulous police work. *A fucking cleat!*

Yes, Abigail had been stepped on by an angry track star. The lesions had become infected. Abigail shook her head and listened. Anyone with even a general understanding of anatomy and medicine could have disproved their theories a dozen ways over, but she didn't argue the point. All that mattered was that the officers had decided she wasn't a drug addict and that her wounds weren't self-inflicted. That meant they would need to investigate. They would need to go to the park.

On the off chance that Abigail's hysterical tale turned out to be true, they brought the whole damn squadron with them.

As the police car Abigail rode in pulled into the park entrance, smoke billowed across the parking lot and engulfed the cruiser in dark gray clouds. The officer driving clicked on the fog lights just in time to avoid a collision with the police car in front of them, which had stopped short. The fire truck whizzed by them on the right, heading toward the ranger station, or what was left of it.

Abigail edged forward in her seat. She squinted out the windshield. It looked as though the fire had started at the ranger station. The building was little more than charred rubble. The flames raged through the woods, with the parking lot acting as a buffer zone, blocking the fire's spread to the west, and the wind direction blocking it from the south. A blaze raged northward into the forest, devouring all life in in its path, reducing lush green and dry brown to cleansing black ash.

Abigail smiled. The fire was burning exactly where it needed to.

Smoked rolled across the lot as the firefighters quickly doused the last smoldering patches in the station. The sun turned the smoke pink and purple where it couldn't shine through. As the smoke began to clear, Abigail took a hard look at the ruins, wondering who or what had started the blaze and whether anyone else had survived. Only a few appliances, including a blackened and tipped-over refrigerator, its door ajar, sat in a mound of soot and cinders.

While everyone fought the blaze, Abigail sat in the patrol car. The officer to whom it belonged had been kind enough to crack open her door before dashing away to help the firefighters. Not for the first time in the last twelve hours, she found herself alone in a place where she had no desire to be.

With hesitant steps, she got out of the car. She slid her shirt up over her nose and mouth, her lungs rejecting the air, which was thick with fumes.

"Over here!" someone yelled.

"He's got a gun!" another shouted.

Abigail ran toward the voices, her hands stretched out in front of her like antennae. Smoke clouds plumed over her, drying out her eyes, then dissipated before the next wave came. In those rare moments of sunshine, Abigail caught glimpses of officers with service pistols raised. As she approached, she saw the man at whom they had taken up arms: a park ranger who looked like he had battled with the Devil and lost.

"Stop!" Abigail yelled. "He's a victim." She flagged down the nearest officer. He seemed hesitant to believe her, a reluctance she understood. Merwin looked like a vagrant, his wiry beard in tangles and full of grime. Thorns and twigs stuck to his clothes. A rifle hung by its strap over his shoulder. Merwin let it slide off his arm and fall to the cement. He raised his hands in the air.

"Stand down," the officer beside Abigail said at last. He gave Merwin a last cursory look then turned to Abigail. "You stay with him. See to it that he gets medical attention if he needs it. We've got to stop this fire from spreading out of control." He holstered his gun and ran toward the fire engine, waving the other officer nearby to follow.

Abigail ran to Merwin, threw her arms around him, and wept. Slowly, he raised his arms and accepted her into them.

"I'm so glad you're okay," she said, her tears washing a circle of dirt from the ranger's shirt.

"Define 'okay.'"

"Well, you're alive, anyway. And it's morning. That has to count for something."

Abigail needed something good to cling to. Karl was dead. There was no changing that. She had to assume the rest of them were gone, too. In Merwin's case, she had been wrong to assume. She wasn't alone. He was her silver lining. Maybe, just maybe, there was still reason to hope.

"I suppose you're right." Merwin smiled, but the movement of facial muscles seemed painful for him, and the smile transformed into a grimace. He closed his eyes and rubbed his neck.

"What happened? Are you hurt?"

"I don't rightly remember. One moment, I was driving us out of here—"

"Us? Are the others all right? Where are they?"

Merwin squinted. He shook his head. "I don't remember. I was with Tyler and Dakota. I must have crashed, or something hit me. The next thing I remember is waking behind the wheel, the car folded against a tree. I've got a whopper of a headache. My skull is rocking harder than Metallica."

Abigail let go of Merwin. She stepped back, eyeballing him for wounds. Her mind conjured an image of the human puppet those things had sent in to destroy the light inside the cabin.

"Are you sure you're okay?"

"Nope, but I might ask you the same thing." Merwin shrugged. "Can't say for certain, but if those things are in my belly, they won't be busting out until the sun goes down, I reckon. Plenty of time for an X-ray."

He pointed at an ambulance. Another had arrived with two more fire engines. "You coming?"

"What are we going to tell them?" Abigail whispered, tilting her head toward the police car.

"What have you told them?"

"Nothing really. I mean, I had no clue how to explain it without them thinking I'm crazy. I just told them someone was killing the campers. I think they all thought I was crazy anyway. I mean, look at me. I'm a mess. But now that you're here, maybe they'll listen to the truth."

"I'll tell them Tyler did it."

"What?"

"They won't believe the truth. They'll believe that. They did the first time."

"What if he's still alive?"

"I reckon we can cross that bridge when we come to it. Somehow, I think that bridge done, well..." He sniffed at the air. "Burned."

"It doesn't seem right, Merwin."

"I know, and I don't like it either. Truth is, if he ain't alive, I hope they never find him. So long as they never find his body, and I'm guessing they won't, it'll keep people out of these woods. No one wants to go where a murderer might be on the loose. Tell them it's a monster, and we'll have all sorts of crazies out here looking for Bigfoot. Even horror stories about giant leeches will only bring out the skeptics and the curious."

Abigail found the plan hard to swallow, but she mulled it over. Keeping the creatures secret, making Tyler a patsy... it all seemed so wrong. But if it kept people away from the park, maybe it was the better course of action. Otherwise, those creatures would continue to feed, and more lives would be lost.

Silence, though, meant that Karl would not be avenged. That stung. "We have to tell someone. Even if yours is the official version, the truth needs telling. We have to tell someone who'll destroy those things."

"Who?" Merwin asked, stroking his beard. "Who is going to come in here and kill giant leeches that nobody else knows exists? Biologists will just want to study them. Hell, they'll probably even seek to protect them as an endangered fucking species. Everyone else will just tell us to go pound tar."

"I'll find someone who will listen. I'll find someone who will do something."

"You do what you feel you must. Me? I'm going to the hospital. I'm going to make up an excuse for them doctors to photograph my insides." He put his arm around Abigail. "You should, too. Come on. We've spent enough time in this place."

As they hobbled toward the ambulance, Merwin using her as a crutch, Abigail watched the spinning lights atop the vehicle. She wanted those for her room, to guard over her as she slept, if she ever dared to sleep at night again.

She smiled and pretended to be okay, but she knew it would be a long time before that were true again. She squeezed Merwin around his waist as her tear ducts threatened to burst. "Well, I know one thing for sure. From here on out, I'll be sleeping with the lights on," she said, trying to lighten the mood and stop herself from crying.

Merwin stroked his beard. "You and me both, Abigail. You and me both."

# EPILOGUE

Life for her had ended and begun at the lake. The park remained empty through the summer, closed as the police searched for the bodies of six people who had gone missing and were presumed dead and for the man the police suspected had killed them. Rumors of something foul, something evil lingering at the lake and hiding there, spread throughout the community and the nearby campus. Wildfires fueled the hysteria and hindered law enforcement's chances of finding anything there except ash and dirt. It seemed that every time firefighters put out one blaze, a new one started in another section of the park.

Authorities suspected arson. They had yet to make an arrest.

No one was allowed into Galveston State Park, but she went anyway. Every day.

"Never have to be alone." Voices rose from the depths. They were always present, always pleading. "Join us."

*I'm here, too,* Tyler's voice spoke inside her head. *I let you escape. I let you live. We care about you.*

She ignored his voice easily enough. Staring out over the still black water, she felt a certain peace knowing those things were trapped below the surface, at least while the sun ran its course across the sky.

*Be here for us,* another voice would say. The creatures were cruel sons of bitches. This voice was harder to ignore, but she had learned to steel herself against it. *We were always there for you, Sis.*

On the side of the lake she had selected that day, nature still thrived. Many innocent creatures lived there, plenty for the evil creatures to feed on. She took a long pull off of her cigarette. Ashes blew in the wind, carried with the voices of those the world would never encounter, not if she could help it.

She flicked her cigarette into the dry brush and walked away.

# ABOUT THE AUTHOR

Jason Parent is an author of horror, thrillers, mysteries, science fiction and dark humor, though his many novels, novellas, and short stories tend to blur the boundaries between genres. From his EPIC and eFestival Independent Book Award finalist first novel, *What Hides Within*, to his widely applauded police procedural/supernatural thriller, *Seeing Evil*, to his fast and furious sci-fi horror, *The Apocalypse Strain*, Jason's work has won him praise from both critics and fans of diverse genres alike. He currently lives in Rhode Island, surrounded by chewed furniture thanks to his corgi and mini Aussie pups.

Curious about other Crossroad Press books?
Stop by our site:
http://store.crossroadpress.com
We offer quality writing
in digital, audio, and print formats.

www.ingramcontent.com/pod-product-compliance
Lightning Source LLC
Chambersburg PA
CBHW020636180626
46816CB00003B/993